The
HIGH
HOUSE

Jessie
Greengrass

Swift

SWIFT PRESS

This paperback edition first published by Swift Press in 2022
First published in Great Britain by Swift Press in 2021

1 3 5 7 9 10 8 6 4 2

Text designed and set in Minion by Tetragon, London
Printed in England by CPI Group (UK) Ltd, Croydon, CR0 4YY

A CIP catalogue record for this book is available from the British Library

ISBN: 978-1-80075-091-3
eISBN 978-1-80075-008-1

Who sang, sea takes,
brawn brine, bone grit.
Keener the kittiwake.

—BASIL BUNTING,
Briggflatts

Sally

I N the morning, I wake earlier than the others. I climb out of bed in my jumper and my socks and I pull on my dressing gown, and after it my leggings and my boots. I go downstairs, and it is cold and dark and very quiet. My boots are beginning to go at the heels, now, but I am trying to get this last winter out of them. My jumper and my leggings are frayed at the cuffs, and my dressing gown is an old blanket with holes cut out for the arms, because dressing gowns are a thing that Francesca didn't think of – and although, between the three of us, we have a reasonable spread of skills, none of us can sew.

In the kitchen, I check the fire in the range, put fresh wood on the embers and open up the vent until it burns. I pour the last of yesterday's well water into the kettle and set it to boil, put dried mint leaves in a mug, make tea. I would have had coffee, once. I think this every morning. I think it, and then I think I can still catch the taste of it, but it's been so long that it could be the taste of anything I am remembering. Milk. Mustard. Ham. They all bring the same flood of saliva into my mouth and the same sad twist into my chest.

Yesterday it rained and I didn't do my coat up properly. Water got in at the collar and I spent the whole day damp, but today I can feel the chill of empty skies and so, I think, it will be clear. Outside, beyond the window, past the orchard, the sky is still full dark, but soon it will start to pale. I open the doors a crack and the air is fresh and cold, and it smells of salt. It will be an hour or more before the others are up. Caro sleeps badly, and often goes into Pauly's room in the night, to lie on the mattress he keeps for her on the floor beside his bed. When he wakes, he will stay still so as not to disturb her. It is his own kind of peace, he says, to lie warm under the blankets in the dark with nothing to do. We take these small luxuries where we can, especially in winter.

You would think that with so much space – with the house and the garden, with the copse and the heath, the dunes and the beach, and only ourselves – it would be easy to be alone, but we are a knot. We cling. Each of us knows, at all times, where the others are, in the same way that we always know what time it is, telling it from some combination of light and shadow and our bones, so that it is only now, when it's early, when Pauly and Caro are upstairs, asleep or still, and things have not quite begun, that I can feel as though I am by myself. I step out through the doors into the garden and, around me, silence spreads. I feel its emptiness. The air begins to lighten. Each breath hangs. I go down through the orchard, through the arch in the hedge, along the path and past the tide pool to where the river spreads, freed now of its cuts and embankments, its holdings and constraints, to make its own slow way into the sea—

Spring is coming. Its mnemonic is in the earth and in the branches, in the greening of the buds, the new spears poking among the dead reeds – and even while the cold still creeps into my clothes, I think of the warmth that will come to chase it, soon. The grass is wet around my ankles. The air is still. From here I can see what is left of Grandy's cottage, and below it the half-gone pub, the village green. The rusting arc of the swing frame rises like a monument. Each year, between water and neglect, less and less of the village remains. Grass grows in tufts from walls. Silt covers gardens. Crabs run across the broken cobbles of the road. I listen to the *pip, pip* of the oys-tercatchers and a solitary curlew's call, and it seems strange to say it, but I am not unhappy. Dawn comes. I turn around and walk back the way that I have come, up the path, away from the river – towards the high house, which is my home.

1

Caro

THE high house belonged to Francesca's uncle, first, but the uncle died not long after she and my father met. He had no children of his own, and so he left the house to Francesca, and the parcel of land that went with it, the orchard and the vegetable garden, the tide pool, the mill. For a long time, the house had been neglected. When I first came here, for summer holidays with Francesca and with father, damp patches spread around the corners of the downstairs rooms. Tiles were missing from the roof. I remember the chill the house had, even in summer, and the way the wind swooped down the chimneys at night. The orchard, outside the kitchen doors, was overgrown, and, beyond it, past the unruly beech hedge with its branch-obstructed arch, the tide pool was choked with reeds. Twice in every twenty-four hours water would flow into the pool, but the sluice gate was long shattered and so, where once the water would have been held to turn the wheel, it only trickled out again as soon as the tide began to ebb. The mill had half-fallen into the mud. The wheel was rotten. It would have been used to grind wheat, when it was built – and now it turns again and powers our generator, which gives us light in winter for as long as we have the bulbs, and runs the fridge in summer. Now, the orchard is carefully pruned. We do the apples in winter and the plums at midsummer, like Grandy taught us, carefully cleaning and sharpening the pruning saw, keeping the secateurs on string round our necks because they are so easy to lose. Now, the hedge is clipped. In the vegetable garden, things grow in rows. There is a greenhouse with all its glass intact. This is what we do, now. We dig and we weed. We plant. We store seed, and we watch the weather carefully for signs of frost. Now, there are hens in the hen coop, although in winter they live mainly in the scullery. We have fields, too, which we have claimed because there is no one else to want them. But when I was a child the orchard and the gardens were overgrown. The coop was empty. The house was dusty and unloved.

i

The high house isn't high, really, but only higher than the land around it, so that when it was first built, before the river had been banked and the cuts made to drain the land, when the rain was heavy and the tide was up and the water spread where it wanted, the house would have been an island, almost, with only the westerly part of its land unflooded, a causeway above the waterline joining the house to the heath. And now at times it is almost an island again.

ii

In those first years, before Pauly was born, after Francesca came to live with me and father, we used to come here for our summer holiday, the three of us spreading out through the rooms of the high house, all into our different places. We were very separate. Francesca worked, up in one of the top rooms, one we use now to store apples, spread in lines across the floorboards, and potatoes in sacks. I roamed the garden, building dens in the honeysuckle which crept across the ruins of the walled garden, decorating my hair with goosegrass, making fairy umbrellas out of coltsfoot leaves. Father stayed in the kitchen. He sat in the old armchair by the French doors, reading, or he stood at the kitchen counter, chopping vege-tables to make lunch. When I was tired of being by myself, I came in from the garden and trailed after him, nagging to be taken somewhere.

—Where, though, Caro?

—The pool, please.

I loved the tide pool, then. Even now, when we are so reliant on it, I regret the loss of its wildness, the way it was before Francesca restored the mill, when reeds grew down close around its edges and small creatures rustled in and out of them, going about their secret business. I loved how still it was, the way the water rose and fell, creeping rippleless up the banks, the way its surface shone when sunlight caught it – but father was afraid of me falling in, or getting caught in the mud, so I wasn't allowed to go near it by myself.

—Oh, all right,

he said, and went to find his jacket and his boots. I waited for him in the orchard, joggling from one foot to the other, until at last he came out to me and we walked through the hedge, down the path which slopes through a sort of meadow, to where the pool is. There, he sat and watched as I swished through the grasses, taking off my shoes to feel the mud suck around my feet, searching for treasures – stones or feathers or once, miraculously, a nest of eggs, each one cracked open where its chick had hatched but otherwise intact, pale blue, speckled, near weightless in the palm of my hand. He watched me until the shadows lengthened to cover the pool entirely, until I started to shiver and yawn, and then he said,

—Home time, Caro. Chop chop.

—I don't want to put my shoes back on.

—Leave them off, then.

I gave him my shoes to carry, and held his hand, and together we walked back to the high house, where Francesca, alone in her upstairs room, kept working.

iii

On other afternoons, father and I went to the beach to dig holes or to throw stones into the sea, the hand-sized flints that stretched like strange eggs along the tideline. Sometimes he let me bury his feet in the sand, or if it was hot enough then he took me into the sea to swim, holding me under the armpits while I splashed. When I thought I felt something touch my foot I screamed, and he laughed, and I clung to him, my arms round his neck and my legs round his waist. I wasn't afraid of the water, then – or if I was then it was a pleasant kind of fear, the sort which sends you yelping with laughter back up the beach when a big wave comes, before you turn and run to chase it out. It was often hot, in July and August when I was a child, although not in the way that it became later, when summers lasted half the year and every day was a white sun in a pale sky. There were lots of holiday lets in the village, and by late morning the section of the beach closest to it would be laid out with people, row after row of them on their backs, or sitting with their children round them, buckets and spades scattered about, and the remnants of picnics, bottles of sun cream, sun hats, spare clothes. Francesca, back in the house, would say,

—How can they stand to enjoy it, this weather?

She didn't have the habit that the rest of us were learning of having our minds in two places at once, of seeing two futures – that ordinary one of summer holidays and new school terms, of Christmases and birthdays and bank accounts in an endless, uneventful round, and the other one, the long and empty one we spoke about in hypotheticals, or didn't speak about at all.

—They act as though it's a myth to frighten them,

Francesca said,

—instead of the imminently coming end of our fucking planet,

and I knew that when she said 'they' she meant father, too, and me.

iv

This was when it was still the beginning of things, when we were still uncertain, and it was still possible to believe that nothing whatever was wrong, bar an unusual run of hot Julys and January storms. All summer I ran, half-naked, through the fine days, and when the weather broke, bringing rains so heavy that the water fell in long ropes through the air, I sat inside the high house and watched it from the window, marvelling at the quantity of it and the force, how it scoured what it touched, washing crisp packets out of hedges, flattening shrubs, cleaning dust – and then, next morning, it would be hot again, but the air would be filled with steam; and the sea, where the river ran into it, stained with mud.

v

We went to the high house at Christmas, too, when some years snow lay on the beach and ice washed in grey sheets down the river, and other years the grass still grew and the leaves had barely turned on their branches. We ate mushroom risotto and then poached pears, and sat by the fire which father had lit, and we opened our presents. No matter what we did, the house seemed to stay empty, with all the doors and windows shut against the cold and so many of the rooms dark, and I tried to make my voice fill up the house while father and Francesca sat on the sofa and read, but there was only one of me and I couldn't make enough noise alone. When the time came to go back to our home in the city it was a relief, because there our lives had formed around us. At home, I knew how to be lonely without it showing. I knew how to occupy myself in my own way, in my own world, which was separate from father or from Francesca – which was private. At home, I knew how to be complete. And then, after a few years, Francesca let the high house out. A young artist lived there for a while. Francesca didn't like her work, which she thought too comfortable,

—As though,

she said,

—there was nothing important to be thought about.

When the artist left, a group of students from a nearby agricultural college moved in, and Francesca let them pay a nominal rent in exchange for renovating the garden.

vi

All that was before Pauly was born, when there were still only three of us. Francesca was not my mother. She loved me but there was no structure to it. I loved her but I was unsure of her. We rarely touched. Father loved us both but serially – first one, and then the other. He couldn't love us both at once because we needed such different things from him. As a three, we were not unhappy, exactly, but we weren't happy, either – and although sometimes it seems to me, looking back, that my childhood ended when Pauly came, I can't say that I regret it. It was too quiet, then, and I was too often alone. It is hard to be a child in isolation. You take on adulthood like a stain.

vii

I was fourteen the day Francesca brought Pauly home from the hospital. Father and I spent the morning cleaning the house, polishing and sweeping and dusting, until every room smelled of beeswax and vinegar. There was a bunch of sunflowers on the table in the hall, stood up in a water jug.

—She'll say we shouldn't have bought cut flowers,

I said, but father replied that just this once she'd like them anyway, which I thought, privately, seemed unlikely. Francesca had been gone a week. The birth had been difficult, father told me, when he came back from the hospital in the middle of the night for a change of clothes. The baby had been positioned awkwardly and for a long time its shoulders had been stuck trying to get free of Francesca's pelvis, and also there had been a loop of umbilical cord round its neck which all the struggle had pulled tighter and tighter so that when at last the baby had been got free, tugged out by a pair of forceps clamped round its skull, it had been blue-grey and limp, and the doctors had taken it straight off, before Francesca and father had even heard it cry, to another part of the hospital to be wrapped in a cooling blanket in case its brain had been damaged.

—The baby is a boy,

father said,

—and we have called him Paul.

Father looked worn out. I made him cups of tea and cooked him pasta with tomato sauce whenever he came home, and I said that of course things would be fine – but to myself I thought that perhaps they would not be fine. I thought of babies in neonatal units, the photos of them I had seen in charity Christmas campaigns or on the news, their tiny bodies old-looking and plugged with wires, barely human, skin like tissue paper spread over bird bones. I thought of the baby, Paul, my half-brother, swaddled in an incubator, and I tried to think of Francesca sat beside him, waiting – but it was impossible to imagine her in such a place. I could not think of her at the mercy of doctors, reaching for a baby that she was not allowed to touch. I could not think of her afraid, but only of her saying to me, when I'd once wanted to know why I wasn't allowed to drink juice from a carton,

—We all have to make sacrifices, Caroline. That is how things are.

No one but Francesca has ever called me Caroline.

viii

When we had finished cleaning, father and I ate lunch, and then we washed up, put everything away, swept up the crumbs. Scrubbed out all signs of ourselves. Father asked if I wanted to go with him to the hospital but I said no, because I was afraid, both of the baby and his birth bruises, and of Francesca, of what had happened to her and of its consequences – that she would either be herself or would be not herself, changed, a strange infant in her arms. Father kissed me, and then he put on his coat and went out to the car. I stood on the doorstep and watched him drive away, and, when he was quite gone, I closed the door behind him and began to wait. I went into the front room, first, where the cushions on the sofa were all undented and every book was slotted into its right place on the shelves. After that I went into the kitchen, where there were no mugs waiting to be washed, and into the bathroom, where the towel hung clean and folded and the soap sat square in its dish. In the room that Francesca shared with father, fresh sheets were tucked neatly beneath the mattress on the bed. The washing basket was empty, its usual tangle of jumpers and tights unpicked, washed and put away. Next door, the baby's room waited, perfect, for a baby. Even my own room was clean, its carpet denuded of books and clothes, its bed made and everything swept, orderly and unfamiliar. I sat at the bottom of the stairs, watching the door, waiting at the centre of all the messless emptiness of our house, and I might have felt unwanted, then. I might have felt that I, too, had been smoothed out, as though father and Francesca had given me up to start again – but really I only felt that I was poised, en pointe. An end had come, but not a beginning, yet – and then, at last, there was the sound of the car, the key in the door. Father stood aside to let them in, Francesca with the baby in her arms, and it was as though not just my brother but both of them were newly born, their fragile skin pinked by first exposure to the sun. I stood in the hallway, feeling the whole world still about me, as Francesca held the baby out to me and said,

—Look, Caroline! This is Pauly—

and I reached out and took him from her, and time began again.

ix

Sometimes, when Francesca went for a shower, she would give me Pauly to hold, and I would watch him, his tiny curving body nestled into the crook of my elbow, his arms and legs waving gently like ropes of seaweed in an underwater current. He felt as though he were a part of me, then, and when he looked at me and I looked back, our matching eyes held wide, I thought

I knew him and he knew me too – until his mouth began to seek, head turning side to side, and his coughing sobs turned into cries and brought Francesca running back.

x

Each morning, father took up residence at the toaster.

—What today, then?

—Two slices, please.

I poured coffee from the pot, one for each of us, and one for Francesca, who came downstairs in her dressing gown, her eyes puffy and face creased, saying,

—Don't ask me how the night was. I feel like I could eat the bloody loaf.

She put the baby in his bouncy chair and sat down next to it, joggling him with her foot so that he tick-ticked up and down, waving his hands in front of his face. In the background, the radio: *…fears for the eastern seaboard of the United States as storms—*

—Turn that thing off, would you?

father called to me and Francesca didn't stop me, although she frowned, said,

—Turning it off won't make it go away—

We poured milk, passed jam. Father took his lunch out of the fridge and packed it in his bag, searched for his wallet and his keys, got ready to leave for his job at the university.

—Another day of students. When will it end—

I peeled an orange and offered it to Francesca, who took it from me, pulled it into segments and ate them, one by one, while Pauly in his chair watched her and made a sort of humming sound.

—Thank you, Caroline.

We had been reconfigured. As a three we were unbalanced, but the baby's weight had evened out the scales. It seemed, at times, as though it were a magic trick done skilfully, so swift and smooth, and I was afraid in case, were I to learn the way that happiness was palmed, the trick would cease to work. Father, buttoning up his coat, said,

—What's today then?

—Double maths,

I told him,

—and French. I hate French.

Francesca picked Pauly up,

—Come on, piglet,

she said to him,

—let's get you into some clean clothes—

and she carried him away from us, back up the stairs, into the soft confines of that cocoon which his room had become.

xi

When I got home from school they were together in father and Francesca's bed, Pauly having his nap and Francesca working, a book in one hand and her notebook open beside her. Pauly, his face pink, his breath even, was draped across her lap and I sat with them, doing my homework on the floor at the end of the bed until Pauly woke, and then Francesca and I played games with him, stacking towers of wooden blocks for him to knock into a heap, pushing toy cars so that their wheels rattled across the floorboards. He liked to be turned upside down, squealing as we took it in turns to dangle him backwards from our laps. I dropped a rubber ball and he watched it bounce down towards stillness. The phone rang. Francesca answered it, and while I sat on the floor opposite Pauly, trying to teach him to clap, I heard her say,

—They think this baby is an admission of defeat,

and then,

—They think it means that I no longer care. Or that I don't believe in what I say—

but watching her I thought that it was not defeat at all. Rather, it was a kind of furious defiance that had led her to have a child, despite all she believed about the future – a kind of pact with the world that, having increased her stake in it, she should try to protect what she had found to love.

It is so hard to remember, now, what it felt like to live in that space between two futures, fitting our whole lives into the gap between fear and certainty – but I think that perhaps it was most like those dreams in which one struggles to wake but can't, so that over and over again one slips back against the mattress, lets the duvet fall and shuts one's eyes. There is a kind of organic mercy, grown deep inside us, which makes it so much easier to care about small, close things, else how could we live? As I grew up, crisis slid from distant threat to imminent probability and we tuned it out like static, we adjusted to each emergent normality and we did what we had always done – the commutes and holidays, the Friday big shops, day trips to the countryside, afternoons in the park. We did these things not out of ignorance, nor through thoughtlessness, but only because there seemed nothing else to do – and we did them as well because they were a kind of fine-grained incantation, made in flesh and time. The unexalted, tedious familiarity of our daily lives would keep us safe, we thought, and even Francesca, who saw it all so clearly – even she who would not let herself be gulled by hope – stood by the open fridge at five o'clock in the afternoon and swore because there was nothing to give the baby for his tea. We fed him fish fingers from the freezer. Father came home. Pauly had his bath, splashed the water with his fists, sucked the flannel, then cried when it was taken away to wipe him. Afterwards, consoled, he was wrapped in a towel to be dried. I kissed him on his damp and rumpled hair.

—Goodnight, Pauly.

Francesca carried him off to bed. Father made dinner and opened a bottle of wine so that a glass was poured, ready, when she came back down, blinking in the light.

—He's asleep at last, thank Christ—

And all the while, outside, the thing that only she could look at straight: the early springs and too-long summers, the sudden, unpredictable winters that came from nowhere and brought floods or ice or wind, or didn't come, so that there was only day after day of sticky dampness and the leaves rotting on the trees and the birds still singing in December, nesting, until the snow came at last and, having overlooked migration, they froze on the branches, and they died.

Francesca, on my laptop screen, was making a speech. Pauly, not yet six months old, was asleep in a sling on her front, his head tucked in beneath her chin, his legs dangling around her waist. She said: *We must recognise that we are being given a final warning – because if we fail to do so, if we fail to act, the consequences will surpass anything we have previously seen, and we will have missed our chance—*

They seemed so much a pair, then, Francesca and Pauly, and as he began to take shape, his personhood unfurling like new green leaves, he grew towards her, reaching out to catch and climb. It was a joy, I found, to watch them. I loved to pick Pauly up when Francesca left the room to fetch something, or to speak on the phone, and to whisper in his ear as he began to fret, *Don't worry, Pauly, she's coming back—*

It seemed miraculous that this tiny almost-person, whose needs were so immediate, whose sense of loss at his mother's absence was so overwhelming, might be so easily restored when Francesca came back and lifted him up onto her hip again. Then his tears would stop at once and he would glare out at the world reproachfully, knotting his fists into her shirt – but nothing lasts. At night the world seems full of edges. The moon, shining through the window, shows up the corners and the breaks. Pauly and Sal think that it is fear which wakes me, which gets me out of bed to go into the garden, to walk beside the river in the dark, but it isn't fear, or not only. It would be so easy, in this green place, to think we had won through – that it was an act of skill or of prescience on our part which had brought us here, in place of all the others who it might have been instead. It wasn't skill. It was only the opportunity Francesca gave to us, and the choice to use it on ourselves. In Pauly's room, before I fall asleep, I stare at his young man's face and try to remember what he looked like as a child, but I have forgotten. I pull the blankets over me and I match my breath to his until, at last, I fall asleep.

xiii

One afternoon, while Pauly had his nap, father and Francesca and I sat on the living-room sofa and watched an island in the mid-Pacific sink. We saw the storm arrive, the cameras picking up the rain, the swelling wind. We saw doors torn from hinges, palm trees bend and give. We watched as an ordinary piazza in a far-off seaside town came apart, its street signs snapped, lamp posts buckled, the café on the corner split open like an egg. Father said,

—At least they knew it was coming.

On the screen, a whole car flew past.

—I mean, everyone had got out already.

Francesca, face taut with fury, stood up and, going into the corner of the room, put both hands against the walls.

—That,

she said, her back to us,

—is very far from the point. And anyway,

she went on, speaking with such fierceness that I thought her words might drill holes through the lath and plaster to let her out of the room, out of our lives,

—there are always some who stay. Why not? Where else can they go? A fucking refugee camp? While the rest of the world argues about who should take responsibility for them? Yesterday they had lives, and now they're just faces in a bloody queue.

—I know,

father said,

—I'm sorry.

—Everybody's fucking sorry—

Next morning, after the storm had moved away, we turned on the television again and saw satellite pictures of the place where the island had been, and where there was nothing now but bare earth and a patch of ocean scummy with debris. The people who had lived there were now in temporary shelters, we were told, on the nearest major landmass, a thousand miles away from where, a week earlier, they had been at home. It was unclear how many had chosen to stay.

In the afternoon, Francesca put her laptop on the kitchen table while she made flapjacks and, sitting with my feet propped up on Pauly's highchair, eating raisins she had spilled, I watched news footage of families hunched under tarpaulins. They looked resigned, as though they already understood what they had become a part of, and I tried to stop myself from crying because I was ashamed of my tears, which were neither compassionate, nor empathic, nor kind, but came because I was afraid, very suddenly and directly, for myself.

It was evening, and Francesca was packing a bag. Father followed her about as she went from room to room, collecting jumpers, chargers, a toothbrush.

—What about us,

he said.

—What about Pauly?

—Paul will be fine.

Francesca slipped her passport into the top pocket of her suitcase. Father said,

—He needs you.

—He has you,

Francesca answered, and she went into her study, and shut the door behind her.

Later, waiting for a taxi, kneeling down to kiss Pauly on his forehead, Francesca said,

—I'm sorry.

It wasn't clear which of the three of us she was talking to.

—If I can help at all – if there's anything I can do – then I have to go.

—Yes,

said father,

—of course, you do.

—I'll be back in a few days. A week, maybe. I have to go. I have to see it for myself. There have to be witnesses.

—Yes,

said father, again.

—We can't just turn our backs.

That night, Pauly wouldn't sleep. He stood at his bed-room door, his face wet with tears and sweat, and howled as though he were in pain. I tried to pick him up, to comfort him, but he writhed and kicked his heels against my legs until I let him go, and so instead I sat next to him, on the brightly coloured carpet, and I whispered to him and kept on whispering,

—It's okay, Pauly, it's okay. It will be okay. I love you. It's okay—

but it was nearly midnight before at last he fell asleep, exhausted, half in and half out of the doorway. I watched him until I was sure he wouldn't wake, and then I carried him to bed. I put on my pyjamas, brushed my teeth, fetched a glass of water, and then, for comfort – his, or mine – I climbed in next to him and, with his small feet pressed against my stomach, I slept, too.

xv

In a newspaper column Francesca wrote:

> *As scientists we are used to remaining in one place. We tell ourselves that it is our job only to present the evidence – but such neutrality has become a fantasy. The time for it is past.*

Every day father went to the university, taught classes, ran seminars. In the evening he came home and marked papers, pursuing his own research in the gaps – and so it was hard not to see Francesca's words as personally directed, a facet of their relationship played out in public. Even then, I knew enough to wince, but there was Pauly to be looked after – and, anyway, perhaps what she had written was less an attack than it was an apology, that she should place the hypothetical, general needs of a population above the real and specific ones of her family. And, anyway, didn't it turn out that she was right.

Towards the end, of course, father went with her – for the last year they were alive, travelling to conferences, emergency committees, summits. I wonder, now, what he must have felt in those last months – what guilt, to have left it too late to change the outcome because he had not wanted Pauly or me to be unhappy. It is the same guilt that I feel now, rooted in the knowledge that I did nothing, in the end, but stay safe at the high house and ride things out. Often, in the night, I wonder how it must have been for them in the last moments, Francesca and father – whether it was slow or quick, a death by falling or one by crushing or by drowning. I wonder how afraid they were. And, sometimes, I think that perhaps they are not gone at all but are still out there, somewhere, working, in a place which is more important to them than here.

xvi

I sat in the garden with Pauly beside me, his hands gripping my shoulder to hold himself upright. I was picking daisies, holding them out to him, just out of reach, making them dance backwards and forwards, their heads nodding, until he squealed with laughter. He squatted down and pulled a handful of grass up by its roots, then held it out to me, his plump fingers curled into a grubby fist around it.

—Thank you, Pauly,

I said, and, taking it, turned it in my hand and offered it back to him.

—Do you want it?

He loved this game, at that age, the back and forth of it – but this time, as he began to reach in turn, he stopped halfway, his gesture interrupted by something he had seen, and instead of taking the grass from me he pointed upwards to a tree and in his brand-new voice said,

—Bird.

I called to Francesca, who had come back from Paris the day before, where she had stood in front of a crowd of university students, all of them dressed head to toe in black, and said *If we are in mourning for anything, it is for a time when we could turn our backs...* Now, she was making bread and when she heard me she came running out through the open kitchen doors, wiping her hands on her jeans, leaving two white trails of flour behind.

—What is it?

she asked.

—What's happened? Has something happened?

—He said 'bird'—

I pointed up into the tree.

—There it is, Pauly,

I said,

—it's still there, look. What's that? What can you see?

but Pauly, quiet again, only smiled at us and held out fists of grass. Francesca said,

—I must get on with lunch,

and, turning away, walked back towards the house.

xvii

Pauly and I were building towers out of wooden blocks and then pushing them over, sitting side by side on the front-room carpet. The door was ajar. On the other side of it, I could hear Francesca moving about.

—Pauly,

I said,

—would you like a story?

I read to him. He sat on my lap and followed the story page by page, and when we found the picture of the wolf Pauly squealed, delighted as I knew he would be, and pointed at the animal's stretched and grinning mouth.

—Big teeth!

he said.

—Big teeth! The wolf!

I heard Francesca's hissed intake of breath. I heard her pause, turn, walk away, and I felt a sudden spasm of guilt. How warm Pauly was in my lap, how comfortable, how soft, and how it must have hurt Francesca then to be in the next room, alone, and to have the truth confirmed: that it wasn't that Pauly didn't talk at all, but only that he didn't talk to her.

In the therapist's office, all three of us sat in a line, Francesca, father, and I. Through the large window in the wall we could see Pauly, playing on a patchwork rug in the next room. He was with the speech and language therapist and she knelt next to him on the floor, where they had built a marble run. Pauly looked calm, I thought. They were playing some kind of game, the woman holding a marble at the top of the run and pointing at Pauly, then letting it go to skitter round the bends and shoot out the bottom, so that Pauly had to run to fetch it. I had worried that people would seem to be judging him, that he would be made to feel that he was at fault, but this might be nothing more than a rather select kind of playgroup. Father and Francesca had been coming here with Pauly for a month, for family therapy sessions. Often, Francesca came back just for this, arriving on the train in the morning and leaving again straight after, so that I was at school the whole time she was home and didn't see her at all, but now it was half term, and they had asked me to come as well. I thought of the others in my class, and what they might be doing which wasn't this – but my life, with Francesca in it, had never been like theirs, and was even less so now, so what would I have been doing? Sitting in the garden with Pauly, perhaps. Taking him to feed the ducks in the park. I didn't like to be apart from him, in case he should want me and find that I wasn't there.

—Sometimes,

the therapist said, breaking the long silence in the room,

—children are a kind of weathervane. They pick up on the currents in family life and … act them out.

—Voice them,

Francesca said, as if explaining things to me, her eyebrows raised.

—Or not.

The therapist smiled, a little thinly, a pale man in a pale sweater with black, square-framed glasses balanced halfway down his stub nose. He looked at me.

—Would you say you are an anxious family?

Afterwards, we went out for lunch. While we waited for our order, Pauly sat on my lap, colouring with crayons on some sheets of paper which Francesca had brought from home. I picked one of his drawings up and turned it over. *An Analysis of Recent Climate Trends and the Increased Likelihood of Devastating Weather Events*, I read. Francesca frowned.

—What they don't seem to understand,

she said,

—is that anxiety is a perfectly reasonable response to what we are living through.

Pauly was drawing people, moon faces with stick bodies underneath, giant feet on the end of dangling legs. Father said,

—But Paul is only a child, and if he is picking up on your – *our* – fears—

He tried again.

—We have to at least try to believe that he will have the chance to live an ordinary life.

Francesca said,

—We have to do no such thing,

and for a moment there was a gap in her fury, and she looked neither fierce nor righteous but only rather sad – as though she could see already how far she had failed, and wished only that the end would come, and let us all out.

xix

In the mornings, on my way to school, I walked Pauly around the corner to nursery, his hand in mine. When we arrived, I took him inside, helped him to take off his coat, watched him hang it on his peg. I gave him his bag and breathed in the nursery smell of boiled carrots, disinfectant and damp clothes. The teachers were kind to me, carefully treating me the same as the real parents – and although the effort showed, I appreciated their making it. In the afternoon father picked him up, dropping in on his way home from the university, or if father stayed late then I would go.

—Where's daddy?

Pauly asked, his eyes wary, his shoulders curled forward.

—It's all right, Pauly,

I said,

—he'll be home in an hour or so. He's teaching. Shall we go to the park?

and his anxiety was forgotten on the swings, where I pushed him back and forth until it was late enough that father would be home.

In the evenings, after Pauly was in bed, father and I sat and watched the news. In Bangladesh the rains had failed. In Japan, there were floods. A delegation from the drowned island had arrived at the UN, seeking restitution. Fires raged through the centre of Australia, and in parts of China the summer was now so hot and humid that it was incompatible with life. Sometimes, cut among the chaos, we saw Francesca, seated in a television studio, a microphone pinned to the lapel of her jacket. Her voice, recorded and reproduced, sounded odd, not unfamiliar but not quite right, as though she were doing an impression of herself.

—I thought she was in Berlin,

I said. We turned the television off and I finished my homework, then went to bed, and when Pauly woke, as he often did, in the small hours of the morning, I let him get in beside me.

—Can I have your arm?

he asked, and I stretched it out across the pillow, for him to rest his head on.

—Time to go to sleep now, Pauly,

I told him, and he did.

xx

It used to be that Pauly needed me, and so I looked after him. I thought it was as simple as a question and its answer, and didn't think about the ways that his small person might be an answer to something in its turn. Now things are the other way about. On bad days, when I can't sit still, when my head aches and I want to sleep but sleep won't come, when my longing for father and for Francesca is so great that I can hardly stand it, then I follow Pauly around. I shadow him.

I know he finds it hard. I know that I should pull myself together.

—Make yourself useful, Caro,

he says, and passes me a spade.

—The effort will do you good.

I start to dig. Sometimes Pauly is right and the digging does help – if not straight away, then later, when I sleep a little better in the night. At other times the digging makes my hands ache and Pauly takes the spade away, and says,

—Why not go for a run, instead?

so I do as he tells me and lace up my running shoes, which we have mended and mended because there are no more pairs left in the barn, and I run out of the high house, out of the orchard and away from the tide pool, away from the things which need doing, away from Pauly and his sideways concern and away from Sally and her worries about what we will eat and how much wood we have stored for the winter, out into the empty countryside, which is quiet and has no interest in me. It is good to be alone when I am running, and afterwards there is a period when I feel better. Pauly waits for me at the high house, and I see his own relief when he sees mine. It is I who need him, now. I need his solidity and his certainty. I need his aptitude for making do. But sometimes, in the night, when I lie on his floor and count my breaths to try and make sleep come, I feel him watching me, and I think that perhaps I have always needed him, even when he was small – even when it looked like it was the other way around, because he gives me shape and substance, and to be needed is to be held in place.

The agricultural students were gone from the high house and it was empty. Francesca began to spend her weekends there – whole weeks, sometimes – and I found it hard not to think that she was avoiding us, Pauly and me. Often, father went with her. I didn't ask what they were doing. The fact of their absence made me angry but it was also, in a way, easier, when they were gone and we were by ourselves. I could relax. The world with just the two of us in it was very small but it was easy. I missed father, but I didn't miss the way I had to make myself seem happy for him, and I missed Francesca, too, but not the feeling she brought into a room that we were all failing against standards that were impossible to match, and not the fear she also brought, the constant awareness of consequences that she would let us neither forget nor ignore. Even father, now, seemed to chafe when he was at home, fidgeting as though he would rather be elsewhere, away with Francesca, and not stuck with us, in our dull routine.

If I thought about it at all then I think that I assumed they must be resting when they went to the high house. I thought that they were being peaceful, just the two of them together, as Pauly and I were peaceful, too, without them. Pauly was nearly four, then, and he was still reserved with strangers but had, when it was only the two of us, the ability to forget himself in joy. In the afternoons, when I had picked him up from nursery, as a pan of pasta sat bubbling on the stove, we lay on the floor of the front room wriggling, pretending to be fish, or we took turns to be lions and hide between the poles of the clothes airer, roaring. He liked to play with the dolls from the doll's house set which I had bought him for Christmas, giving each of them a different voice, making them chatter to one another, bicker, fall out, make up, console. On Saturday mornings, after we had done the shopping, he liked to make biscuits, cracking eggs two thirds into a bowl and one third across the table, sticking his fingers in the sugar jar when he thought I wasn't looking—

—We won't do baking if you eat the sugar, Pauly—

He liked to play hide-and-seek, but could never get the hang of staying hidden and would leap out as soon as I came into a room, shouting,

—Here I am, Caro! Here I am—

Things were so simple when I was with him that it made those moments when the outside world intruded seem extraordinarily violent. Sometimes, when I went into the corner shop to buy bread or milk, I would catch sight of the front page of a newspaper and be surprised by photographs of people knee-deep in mud, of children lying in rows on mattresses, their eyes huge in their skulls, and I would feel a sudden sickening terror, a lurch, and I would shut my eyes. That was how it felt, outside: that there was something always waiting, just beyond the edge of vision, to terrify or to reproach. Inside, with Pauly, when it was just the two of us, I was safe – or I felt safe – or I could turn away from what I was afraid of. I was six months shy of my eighteenth birthday, and in my last year at school. Around me, it seemed, the world sank, or froze, or burned. I had no idea what I would do next, and when I thought about it – when I thought about anything other than Pauly, and the minutiae of our lives together – I felt only terror, which shaded into fury at its edges.

xxii

Francesca came home for a few days to work at the university. In her presence, Pauly was muted. He watched her. She became even more than ordinarily busy, cramming into the few days what would otherwise have taken weeks – cooking stews and pasta sauces for the freezer so that we would eat acceptably when she was gone; planting runner beans in the garden; tying up the raspberry canes in rows; repainting the front door where Pauly had scratched it with a wooden duck on wheels. I wished that she would go away again. I missed the days when we ate honey toast for tea instead of vegetables. I missed the stop-start bustle of the mornings and the evening winding-down, Pauly in the bath saying, *Will you get in with me, Caro?* while I sat beside him, ready with a towel – and then the stories, the goodnight kiss, the sudden quiet when he was asleep but the house was still so full of him that I didn't feel lonely at all. I missed him creeping into bed beside me, and waking in the night to find his feet pressed into the small of my back. I missed the struggle to get him dressed in the mornings, his legs and arms multiplying and going in all directions. When Francesca was there, she said,

—Put on your trousers now please, Paul,

and he did, each foot straight into each leg. She took him to the bathroom, brushed his teeth, stood over him while he washed his hands.

—I'm taking you to nursery today.

Pauly nodded. I followed them, trailing behind, checking inside Pauly's nursery bag to make sure he had his book, spare pants, a snack. Francesca knelt down to put his wellies on, her back to me.

—He likes to have his trousers tucked into his socks,
I said,

—otherwise his socks fall down,

and I saw her shoulders set, her neck tense. It gave me such pleasure to hurt her.

xxiii

Shame comes from nowhere. It is like sheet ice my thoughts run onto, unseen in advance and then unbalancing, so that I sprawl and slide – but it seemed to me, then, that Francesca had measured her love for Pauly by the extent to which she could fix him. Then, when it turned out that he could not be fixed at all because he wasn't really broken – was only a small boy who felt afraid at times because we were all afraid – she had put him to one side, and she had put me aside, too. I was angry that she didn't want us. I was angry that she refused to protect us, bringing into the house with her when she came the thought of all the things I wished to avoid, and then leaving again, an endless series of taxis to and from the station.

All the time that she was away, at the high house, with father, I thought that it was because they were happier without us. I didn't know that they were busy there, clearing the tide pool, fixing the sluice gates, installing the generator. I didn't know that they were stocking the barn with supplies. I only knew that, when they came back, they brought fear with them, tracked in like mud across the carpet.

xxiv

I left school for good at lunchtime on the day I turned eighteen. I walked home. The house was empty. I had no plans, either for the afternoon or for the time beyond it – my life, which stretched empty ahead. Or didn't. It was becoming clear to everyone, now, that things were getting worse. The winter before, half of Gloucestershire had been flooded, and the waters, refusing to recede, had made a new fen, covering homes and fields, roads, schools, hills rising from it like islands. In York, the river had burst its banks and the city centre was gone, walls which had stood for nearly two millennia washed halfway down to Hull. People didn't say these places were gone. They didn't say that there were families living in caravans in service stations all along the M5, lined up in the car parks with volunteers running aid stations out of the garage forecourts. People said,

—They must have known their homes were vulnerable—

We were protected by our houses and our educations and our high-street shopping centres. We had the habit of luck and power, and couldn't understand that they were not our right. We saw that the situation was bad, elsewhere, but surely things would work out, because didn't they always, for us? We were paralysed, unable to plan either for a future in which all was well, or one in which it wasn't.

—I'm not going back,

I said to father, when he came home from work because the school had called to tell him I had left.

—What will you do instead?

he asked, and I shrugged one shoulder up and slid my eyes away. There had been daffodils in the park at Christmas. The coast path had been redrawn at six different places over the last three years.

—I have to go and pick Pauly up from nursery,

I said,

—unless you're going to do it,

and I walked down the road to where Pauly was waiting, standing at the gate in his coat and hat and mittens.

—Your shoes are on the wrong feet,

I said.

—No, they aren't.

—Oh well, if you say so. What did you have for lunch?

—I can't remember. Strawberry sponge for pudding.

—Tasty. I love you, Pauly.

—I love you too. Can I watch a film when we get home?

—No. Pasta pesto for tea.

He took my hand, and worry burned off like mist.

xxv

That evening, Francesca came home. I don't know where she had been, but she smelled of mould and filthy water and she was exhausted. She looked thin. After Pauly was in bed I sat with her and father at the kitchen table.

—What will you do?

father asked me again, and Francesca said,

—That's a pretty stupid question, under the circumstances.

Father let his breath hiss out between his teeth. He said,

—We can't just give up on everything.

—Of course not,

Francesca said – and then, turning to me,

—Anyway, we need you to look after Paul.

So then I knew how absolutely she had given up.

xxvi

Later, unable to sleep, I went downstairs to fetch a book, and, standing in the hall, I heard them talking, father and Francesca together. The door was slightly open and I watched them through the crack it made. They were still sitting at the kitchen table, just as I had left them, side by side, facing my empty chair. Father asked,

—Are you so sure?

—Yes,

Francesca replied,

—I am. I think I am. We always knew a tipping point would come. It's a surprise, really, that it's taken so long.

—You could stop,

father said.

—If there's no point. We could stay together, for a while at least. Caro is unhappy. Paul too, probably, although I agree it's harder to tell.

They were silent for a long time, then, and I stood very still in the corridor and thought of Pauly, the way his body twitched in his sleep, the tense look he got when Francesca was there, and how it was not hard at all for me to tell if he was happy or not. At last, Francesca said,

—I might be wrong.

There was more silence, and I waited. Father said,

—We could be a family—

When Francesca spoke again her voice was sharp and pointed as an awl.

—At least this way,

she said,

—they'll both be safe.

The next morning, when I went downstairs, father was in the kitchen drinking coffee, and Francesca was gone.

—She had an early flight,

he told me.

—She said to say goodbye.

—To me,

I asked,

—or to Pauly?

—Both. Of course, both—

Pauly, bounding down the stairs, ran straight towards me, calling,

—Caro! Caro! I dreamed I was a robot!

The day began.

xxvii

Pauly only went to nursery in the mornings now, to give me time to tidy, do the washing, get the shopping. I picked him up just before lunch and took him home, walking the short distance hand in hand, stopping to look at things that caught his interest, at leaves and beetles, car number plates, discarded crisp packets.

—Oh, Pauly. Please don't pick that up. It's filthy.

—But Caro, it's *green*—

For lunch we ate sandwiches, then washed up together and went to the park. Played on the swings. Came home. Ate tea. Played. Bath. Stories. Bed. When he was asleep the washing, ironing, hoovering. Every day the same. And, in the routine of it, I found that I had misplaced my fear. The future was only the weeks until half term, when there would be planned trips to museums, city farms, the cinema, then back to nursery again. Things had a form and, carried along by it, the future ceased to seem important, although I knew that it would still happen to us, coming on while I was cutting carrots for snacks, while we fed oats to the ducks, played tag, stuck plasters to grazed knees. I fitted my life to Pauly's, because he needed me – or because I needed him, the way he looked me full in the face and smiled, the excuse he gave me: that I could not possibly be anywhere else, because I was here. This is the absurdity of it – that I couldn't forgive Francesca because she chose the world over Pauly, and now I can't forgive myself because I didn't. I'm no longer angry with Francesca. Somewhere in the miles and miles I ran between the high house and the river, the river and the sea, I found that I had come to understand what it was she had tried to do, but who is there left to do the same for me? What option is there, in the end, for those few of us who have survived, but to be the unforgivable, and the unforgiven? All those who might have lived instead of us are gone, or they are starving, while we stay on here at the high house, pulling potatoes from soft earth.

xxviii

The spring before Pauly and I came to the high house, Francesca and father were away almost constantly and it was hot, from the last week of February right through March and April, into May, every day high and clear and bright like a remembered summer, except that it wasn't summer. In the afternoons, Pauly played naked in the garden, poking in the bushes to find insects or pouring water on my feet from the watering can while I squealed and laughed at the cold. I wore Francesca's big sun hat, and when we went out, both of us in shorts and sandals, we ran through the sliver of shade the houses made on the pavement and felt the warmth come up from the ground to meet us. We knew that it was fever heat, a sign of illness, the air too thin and the cement on the ground too thick, the whole city a storage heater, but still we couldn't help but feel ourselves stretch up towards it, the sun, which reached into our bodies and softened them like wax. People stopped work early to lounge in parks. Children sat on doorsteps sucking freeze pops. On buses, passengers smiled at one another. There was such joy in it, the light and warmth, as though we had escaped the winter. Pauly and I went on day trips, into the forest to the east of the city to feel the trees make their own cool, or west, to swim in the river. Away from the pavements, the acres of concrete, the heat was less pronounced. Away from people, it was easier to maintain the fiction of normality – but in the long grass of a deer park we searched for grasshoppers and there were none. The hum of bees was missing. The birds were quiet. I took Pauly to a place I remembered going to with father, once, where there was a greengage tree. I remembered father lifting me up above his head so that I could pull the soft fruit from the branches, and I remembered how sweet it had tasted, juice running down my wrists – but now the tree was bare, its branches brittle, its leaves a brown carpet across the dry ground.

xxix

I lay in the big bed with Pauly curled up next to me, asleep. The window was open to let in what breeze there was and I heard the city sounds which came in with it, the hooting and the roaring of traffic, the wailing of sirens, the rattle of trains. Somewhere, a party was happening. I heard the steady thumping of the bass, an occasional bark of laughter. Someone shouted something indistinct. Beside me, my phone rang, an overseas number. I picked it up, climbing swiftly out of bed and leaving the room so that I didn't wake Pauly when I answered it—

—Hello?

—Caro? It's me. It's dad.

He sounded tired. It was five hours behind where he and Francesca were, on the east coast of the US, so it could only have been early afternoon, but perhaps they had been up all night, sat round a table in a conference centre trying yet again to force understanding where it wasn't welcomed. I said,

—Dad!

and heard him sigh.

—I'm sorry, but we're going to be here longer than we thought. I—

I sat down at the top of the stairs and leaned my head against the wall.

—I'm sorry,

he said, and sounded it.

—What's happening?

I asked, but instead of an answer, he said,

—I want you to take Paul to the high house. Pack your bags now. Leave in the morning. Okay? First thing. Get the early train—

—What's happening? What's going on—

From somewhere in the space behind him I heard a click, the sound of a door opening, a voice calling his name—

—Yes, soon,

he said, to someone else, and then to me he said,

—I have to go. I love you, Caroline. I love Pauly, too. Tell him—

Then clear across the space between us, before the line went dead, I heard Francesca say *There isn't time*—

45

I stayed where I was, sitting on the staircase in the dark, until I was sure that he wouldn't call again, and then I went back into the bedroom where Pauly, fast asleep, had turned himself to lie in a star shape across the full width of the bed.

xxx

While Pauly slept, I packed a hiking rucksack, stuffing it with handfuls of pants, with T-shirts and socks, toothpaste, toothbrushes, soap. Pauly had his own suitcase, a ladybird on wheels which doubled as a kind of seat, and into that I packed his raincoat, his wellington boots, some toys. I made sandwiches for the journey and put them in a shoulder bag. I didn't pack a photograph of father. I didn't pack the necklace that had been my grandmother's, or the card that Pauly had made me for my birthday the year before – but then, what good would those things have been, even had I thought to bring them? I wish I had packed the *Penguin Book of English Verse*. I wish I had packed a garlic press. I wish I had the scissors that Francesca used to cut Pauly's hair.

xxxi

Before I went back to bed, creeping quietly in beside Pauly, gently nudging his warm feet away from my side, I went downstairs and switched on the television. A hurricane that had been building in the Caribbean had veered west, suddenly, and was now projected to hit Florida sometime in the next few hours at a strength so high that it lacked any current designation. Weather conditions in the area were already difficult, bordering on extreme. Evacuation was advised, but might be impossible.

—How is it,

a man in a suit, sat in a television studio, asked,

—that so little warning has been given?

and the woman opposite him, whose hair was not quite smooth, whose blouse was rumpled, as though she had dressed hurriedly, her mind elsewhere, answered,

—These conditions are unprecedented. We have no models appropriate to this situation.

—So are you saying,

the man pressed her,

—that we are now looking at a future in which we no longer have fair warning of extreme weather events?

—Yes,

the woman said,

—that is exactly what I am saying.

xxxii

It didn't occur to me that Francesca would not be safe, and I assumed that father would be, too, because he was with her. Francesca was important. She would be looked after. There would be some plan, I thought, or there would be a refuge or a bunker – and then, afterwards, I thought that perhaps this had been her intention all along, now that her other hopes were lost: to show how such exemptions, so long taken for granted, no longer held. None of us, now, would be let off, not even her – no power, no wealth or name or habit of ease would save us in the end – except that all the time, all through those last months and weeks, she had been building an exemption for Pauly, so that he, unlike everyone else, would be kept safe. We are all at the mercy of the weather, but not all to the same extent.

xxxiii

In the morning, I got Pauly dressed, ate breakfast. When Pauly went to wash his hands I checked the news, but could find out only that the storm had hit, with what seemed to be extraordinary violence, and that its epicentre had been on the district of the city where Francesca and father were staying. I had no message from them. Pauly was in a bad mood – contrary, bolshy – and so it was easy, as I fought to get him to eat his toast, to get dressed, to put his shoes on, to ignore my worry and think only about ourselves.

—But I don't want to go away,

he said, his voice a whine.

—We have to, Pauly.

—Why? Why do we?

—Because father told us we had to. It'll be an adventure.

—It won't.

—All right then, it won't, but we still have to go, so put your shoes on.

At the bus stop, Pauly sat on his wheeled suitcase, pushing it in circles with his feet. We got on the bus, got off it. We went into the station. The concourse was very busy. I left

Pauly standing with our bags by a pillar next to a sandwich shop and went to buy our tickets, trying hard, as I waited in the queue, not to look at the large screen above the departure boards where rolling news showed footage of trees bending in the wind, waves breaking across an esplanade. There were still three quarters of an hour left until our train was due to leave. I took Pauly to a café, where we drank smoothies from plastic bottles and ate pain au chocolat that came in little bags, and I can still feel it in my mouth, even now – the cheap, oily chocolate and the doughy pastry wrapped around it, packet-stale, familiar. Pauly didn't want to finish his, so we left it on the table when our platform was called – and it seems extraordinary to think how profligate we were. How careless. We were so unaware of all we had to lose, and how long has it been, now, since we had any bread except the flat, heavy loaves that Pauly makes, sometimes, from the wheat we grow and grind ourselves? How long has it been since we could leave even the worst food behind, uneaten?

—Come on, Pauly,

I said,

—hurry up. We don't want to miss it.

We made our way across the busy concourse, found the platform, found the train. Found seats. Sat down.

xxxiv

Station by station the train emptied. We ran east into the tail end of the morning and then into the afternoon, rattling through the outskirts of the city, through its hinterland to what lay beyond, a succession of small towns with bunting strung across their streets giving out to fields, to woods, to the curve of a river and children standing on a white painted bridge, a village with a fete, a farm with horses. Pink houses sat alone between hedges. Unfamiliar stations stood undisturbed. By the end there was only us and one other woman, who sat two seats in front of us and turned to stare at me. Pauly breathed a cloud onto the window and used his finger to draw faces in it.

—Stop it, Pauly,

I said, more sharply than I meant because I felt the woman's judgement on me, but it wasn't Pauly's fault that he was bored, and at once I was ashamed.

—Sorry, Pauly. I didn't mean to snap.

He stood up on his seat.

—Sit down,

I said, and he flopped back again, crossing his arms and sulking until he saw a white bird from the window.

—Look, Caro! An egret!

—Is that a good one?

I asked, and he nodded.

The winter before, Pauly had found a bird spotter's guide-book on the shelves at home and since then he had spent hours looking at it, making me read out the names of the birds, their identifying features, the descriptions of their eggs – but whereas this information had left my mind, running out of it like water, Pauly had stored it, reproducing details at will.

—They're a kind of heron,

he said.

—Oh, isn't it beautiful—

and it was, pale as a ghost and tall and still at the edge of a lake. We watched it out of sight.

At the last stop but one the other woman got off and we were alone.

—Us next, Pauly,

I said.

—We're nearly there.

We stood up. I took down our things from the luggage rack. The train slowed, stopped, running to the buffers, and we got out, stretching our legs on the empty platform, and everything around us was perfectly still in the baking sun.

XXXV

The town was eight miles inland from the high house, another half from the village where the road ran, and I had thought that we would get a taxi, but it was early on a weekday afternoon and the station was empty and so was the street outside. There were no people, and no cars on the road. I checked my phone, but there was no internet connection. The station had no ticket office, only a machine to put your card in and a window with a blind drawn down. There was a note pinned to a board with the number of a cab firm, but when I called it there was only the steady monotone of a disconnected line. The air shivered with heat. There was a smell of dust and lavender.

—We can get a bus,

I said to Pauly, my voice shrill with the effort of sounding unconcerned, but when I checked the timetable I found that the next bus wouldn't be until the following day. I made a heap

of our bags in the shade of the awning above the station door
and left Pauly sitting on them.

—Don't move,

I told him,

—I'll try and find a cab office. I won't be long.

I walked as quickly as I could around the nearby streets,
but there was no cab office and I was afraid to leave Pauly too
long in case he wandered off, or someone came and found
him. I went into the post office, where a woman sat behind
the counter, scrolling on her phone.

—Excuse me,

I asked,

—but do you have the number for a taxi?

The woman shrugged, barely looking up, and gave me a
number, different to the one I had found in the station, but
when I called it, although it rang and rang, no one answered.

—No one's picking up,

I said.

—What shall I do? I have a child with me.

The woman shrugged again.

—Try the pub, I would,

she said.

—The landlord's son does lifts sometimes.

I found that I was close to crying. It was only the thought
of Pauly waiting for me that made me swallow my humili-
ation and go into the pub next door, where it was cool and
dim and a handful of men sat round tables, glasses cupped
in their hands, staring up at a television screen on which a
photograph of Francesca was superimposed above video

footage of a hotel with its front wall ripped open. Through the hole I saw beds, wardrobes, sofas. The camera panned, and I saw twisted metal sticking out like broken bone from split concrete. Brown water, scummed with wreckage, swirled in and out of restaurant windows. *Environmental activist and academic feared dead*, I read, from the text that scrolled along the bottom of the screen, *in unprecedented storm—*

—Can I help you, love?

someone asked, but he was very far away indeed, it seemed, and anyway I had no answer. I turned, and went back into the street, back into the sunshine, back to the station where Pauly sat on his suitcase, kicking his heels against the pavement.

—I can't find a taxi,

I said.

—We'll have to walk—

and, trusting, uncomplaining, he looked at me, stood up, smiled.

—Is it a long way, Caro?

—Not too far.

We started to walk.

xxxvi

Sometimes, on the cusp of sleep, I can still hear them, father and Francesca. Father says, *I love you, Caro*, and Francesca, interrupting, calls, *There isn't time—*

It was extraordinary how quickly things fell apart, in the end. That city which, a day earlier, had been impregnable, glinting bright with glass and power, was swallowed by the sea.

The land it had been built on would not be given back. Father and Francesca would not be given back. All these things were forfeit, and, along with them, the sense we'd always had that, whatever happened, we would be all right.

xxxvii

We followed the river out towards the sea, first through the outskirts of the town, past the newbuild housing estates and the playgrounds, the primary school, the supermarket with its car park, the drive-through fast-food restaurant and the petrol station. Pauly walked beside me, holding my hand.

—I'm thirsty,

he said, and I gave him some of the water that was left in the bottle, tepid from lying in my bag in the sunshine. At first, the path was tarmacked and the river in its well-cut bed ran slow and brown, but soon we were out into fields, green beet tops and maize, and wheat. The river widened. There was an embankment, and we walked along the top of it, the path becoming narrower and runnelled. My rucksack was heavy. Pauly slowed to a trudge in front of me, his suitcase bouncing along behind him on its small wheels, sticking in the tufty grass. He stumbled, and stumbled again.

—You're doing really well,

I said.

—It's not far now—

but really I didn't know how far it was. The sun was hot. I thought that I could smell the sea. The fields ended and there was a heath, and then a wood. Pauly began to cry.

—I'm too tired, Caro. My feet are sore.

—Sit down here for a bit, then,

I told him.

—Have a rest. I won't be long.

Leaving him cross-legged on the path, I took the bags and walked with them away from the river, scrambling down the side of the embankment into the trees, pushing through the thicket of new growth at the wood's edge, whippy saplings rising out of brambles, to where the old oaks were, their trunks split low, their lichened branches growing long and hanging into one another. I stuffed my bag into the bowl of one so that it would be held off the ground and might, with luck, stay dry, and balanced Pauly's suitcase on the top of it. When that was done I stood for a moment, surrounded by the forest sounds, the rustlings and scurryings, the songs of innumerable birds, and wondered how I would go on – but what else could I do? I turned and made my way back to the path, where Pauly with his tear-stained face was waiting, and I picked him up and set him on my back, his hands around my neck, mine beneath his legs. I walked again, one foot in front of the other, and I didn't think of father then, or of Francesca, but only of the burning in my legs and spine, the ache like heated wires in my arms, the sharp ground underneath my feet, and time was gone. The world was gone. There was only Pauly left, and me, and the path. I never went back for the bags.

It was approaching dark by the time I saw the sea, a thin grey line on the horizon, and Pauly had fallen asleep, his head resting loose on my shoulder. The river was very slow now, and on each side of it there was meadowland, green and empty, and above it the vast sky – and then, at last, there was the path I recognised, leading away from the river and down among the reeds, where wooden boards were slung across the many small channels which stood at intervals, cutting this way and that, their water still and dark and deep. The first stars were out. Each step made me wince with effort but finally we reached the tide pool, and then I saw for the first time that it had been cleared, no longer the scrub that I remembered. Beyond it, the yew hedge which marked the boundary of the orchard was neatly pruned. I was too tired to be surprised. I went through its arch, and found that where I had been expecting a garden run to seed and a house that was shuttered, dark, there was lush grass between the apple trees and light spilling out through the windows of the house. A girl walked towards me. She had come out to meet me from the house, and when she reached me she lifted Pauly from my back, gently so she didn't wake him, and then she was walking on ahead of me, and I was following her, back through the garden, into the house – and that is how we came here, and we have never left.

2

Sally

WHEN I was six years old, I ran away, setting off alone along the lane which led from Grandy's cottage to the heath, carrying my old brown suitcase. I went against the flow of people who filed down the hill into the village, trippers on their way to wander past the church, to pick flowers from front gardens and drop ice-cream wrappers round the swings, to lean over the harbour wall and lie in rows along the beach. My suitcase was unwieldy, and heavy because I had packed it with everything I had thought I might need – a jumble of toys, my best pink frock, my towel with the hood made to look like a rabbit's face – and its edges banged against my leg as I walked. I reached the old schoolhouse and turned onto the footpath which skirted the top of the marshes, carrying on until I broke out of the woody scrub and into the open. The sun shone. Rabbits cropped the turf. I was wearing my party shoes because I hadn't wanted to leave them behind and couldn't fit them in the suitcase, but they were hard, with stiff soles, and rubbed the skin to blisters on my toes and the backs of my heels.

When I reached the place where Grandy and I went for picnics on sunny days, a sort of bowl in the turf where an oak tree grew, its branches long and low to dapple shade across the ground, I sat down and ate the two chocolate biscuits which I had stolen from the pantry shelf. Chocolate smeared itself across my face and fingers. I hadn't brought anything to drink and the biscuits and the walk had made me thirsty. The air was hot. I was tired. My feeling of defiance had evaporated. I took my grubby blanket, remnant of babyhood, out of my suitcase and lay down on the grass, rubbing its soft fabric against my cheek. There was the sound of insects, the smell of gorse. I fell asleep.

I had woken up by the time Grandy came and was sitting next to my suitcase, waiting for him. It was halfway through the afternoon and I was crying because I was hungry.

—Here you are,

he said, and picked me up, carrying me home in his arms, my suitcase held in two crooked fingers, my head resting on his shoulder, swaying with each stride.

—Grandy,

I said,

—I was running away.

—Yes, Sal, love. I know.

At home, Grandy put me in the bath and then to bed, dressed in a fresh nightie and tucked under a clean sheet, as though I were unwell, and I lay quiet in the peculiar underwater light of a shaded room on a bright day and listened to him move about downstairs. The window was open. I smelled the summer garden. I heard the bees, the hooting of wood pigeons. A car started up. Grandy closed a door. I slept again.

i

Grandy was a caretaker of sorts. He looked after the village, which, in the fifty years or so since he had sat on the green and listened, he told me, to the men outside the pub argue about whether the fishermen had it worse than the farm labourers or the other way about, had altered until, by the time I started school, it was made up almost entirely of second homes or holiday lets, cottages you could spend a fortnight in, nine straight miles from the supermarket, longer on the winding road. Grandy kept things going when the people who owned the houses were elsewhere. He did the gardens. He put out the bins. He cleared the gutters and watched the roofs for missing slates. He painted the frames of the sash windows to keep the rot at bay and swept up the fallen leaves in autumn so that they didn't turn to sludge, storing them in bags, carefully marked with their year of collection, until they rotted down to a fine, black mould, which he spread back on the earth each spring. After the storms which blew up from the sea in autumn and winter he went out collecting firewood, taking a chainsaw to fallen branches, loading them up on the trailer of the quad bike he rode until he said he was too old for it.

—Waste not want not, Sal,

he said, giving me a bag to put the smaller twigs in for kindling.

—Make sure you leave some where they are, mind. Woodlice need homes as do the rest of us, and we're not so desperate these days that we must take it all.

At weekends and in the holidays I went with him, wherever he was going, and I helped, or got in the way, or lay on soft lawns and read while he worked. The village was his. It was he who looked after it. The apples which ripened in September in all the trees in all the gardens were Grandy's, and the pears, and he stored them in whichever sheds had room for them, laying them side by side in rows, not touching, so he could go back for them as he wanted through the winter – and he made cider, plastic bins of pulp fermenting in his own shed to be strained, later, through old pillowcases hung from a hook in the kitchen roof. The results were poured into demijohns and kept in the airing cupboard for the winter. If you stood outside the cupboard, even with the door shut, you could hear them, bubbling softly away to themselves. It was always a comforting sound.

In the evenings, after tea, we sat together on the bench in the garden which looked down across the lawn to the herb patch, or in winter by the stove, and he listened to me do my reading.

—Bath time, then,

he said when I was done, and fetched a towel and my pyjamas while I splashed about, pretending that my knees were islands. I went to bed.

—My turn to read,

he said, and did the voices, even when I told him not to.

ii

Once a fortnight in summer Grandy mowed the grass in the churchyard. I lay beside the yew tree, watching clouds scud across the sky above the church spire.

—Hi ho, Sally!

Grandy called, as he puttered past on his ride-on lawn-mower, pretending that it was a horse.

iii

Standing among the graves when he had finished mowing, Grandy pointed out a few which had our name on them, or corruptions of our name, and I read the inscriptions – those sad, small indications of lives lost: *died aged 77, devoted father and husband*; *my beloved wife, aged 42, may the angels commend you*; *a daughter, born 4th April, died 6th June*; *on the 22nd October he passed beyond us, taken by the sea—*

—Pity the poor buggers,

Grandy said, and then, as though by way of an apology,

—Precarity and continuity, Sal. We all end up dead, but the land we leave goes on, we hope.

iv

In summer, people came to wander through the churchyard or swing on the lychgate. They sat down to do up their laces in the porch, or to eat their sandwiches, leaving crumbs between the flagstones and wrappers slotted into the collection box.

—A bit of common respect wouldn't cost them anything,

said Grandy to the vicar, who was his friend.

—Ah well,

the vicar responded,

—who are we to judge.

—Well you're the vicar, for one thing,

Grandy said,

—and then again, it's me who has to sweep up the crumbs,

and they both laughed at their joke.

The foundations of the church dated from the eleventh century, although all that was above them had been destroyed by fire and rebuilt early in the sixteenth, when the tower was raised and the ceiling rafters carved and painted. It is still standing now, its feet above the waterline, where it had been built to be a refuge, for bodies as much as for the souls that were housed within them. It's my place, now. The key to its door, made of black iron and as long as my hand, its barrel as thick as my thumb, is kept in the middle drawer of the dresser in the high house and I take it out when I want to be away from the others, from Pauly and from Caro. Then I walk up the river to the far bridge, above the new high-water mark, and cross over to the other side. When I get to the church, I let myself through the door and it is a different kind of quiet, once I am inside, to that which has settled everywhere else. This has accrued for so long that now it is beyond silence, and there is no sadness in it. It is not like the quiet of the village, or what is left of it, which is the silence of absence, the inaudible clanging of all we have lost.

I don't believe in god, but I believe in this building which has endured, which has been sustained by all those who have come here, as I come here – each pair of hands polishing the altar rail, each pair of feet treading the stone, wearing it so that the flags have become dished in the centre. I do my part, as they did theirs. I keep the floor swept. I bring hedgerow flowers and a jar of fresh well water each week to set on the altar steps. This was a place of pilgrimage, once – the end point of a walk which followed its founding saint's footsteps eastwards. When I was a child here with Grandy, people came in dribs and drabs throughout the year, and then in floods at Easter, most of them in walking shorts and stout boots, but some came barefoot, or in habits and knotted belts. The rest were tourists, who stood in the knave with their guidebooks and looked up at the rafters, at the wooden angels which hover, their wings outstretched, their ancient faces looking down, the gold leaf on their trumpets and their flight feathers still just visible in the light coming through the plain glass chancel window. The church was in use, then. Communion was held once a month but evensong was weekly, and often visiting choirs would come to sing, although Grandy and I were its only standing congregation.

v

Before services the vicar would often come to the cottage, and he and Grandy would walk around the garden together, peering at the plants, inspecting the state of the vegetables.

—It's a good year for broad beans, vicar. And see here, look at these lettuces.

—Well, of course,

the vicar told him,

—you have the time for it,

and Grandy laughed, his head thrown back.

Afterwards we walked up the lane together, all three of us, and if the weather was fine we might take the longer route, along the river to the bridge and then across the heath, curving back down to enter the churchyard through the gate, and then to go our separate ways – the vicar to the vestry, I into a pew to read while I waited, and Grandy, who was both sexton and ringer, to the bell rope where he would call, he said, one of his eyebrows lifted, the righteous in to prayer.

—And will they come?

I asked.

—In this rain?

Grandy said,

—Not likely,

and he went off, chortling to himself.

vi

The summer I turned five, Grandy taught me to swim. We went down to the beach on still days and waded out into the water until Grandy was waist-deep and I was up to my shoulders, and then he said,

—Go!

and I launched myself, Grandy's hands around my middle to keep me from going under, my flailing legs and arms turning the water to foam.

—Kick! kick! kick!

he shouted.

—Kick, Sal, kick!

and I tried, but for weeks all I could manage was a slow flounder, until one day I hit some sweet spot of strength and buoyancy and found myself afloat. After that we often swam together. Grandy liked to go every day, unless the sea dragged too fiercely to be safe, and even then he would wade out into it, standing thigh-deep in churning water, leaning against the waves which tugged and sucked, trying to pull his legs from under him. He went in the middle of winter, even, plunging all at once into the icy water so that, he said, he didn't have time to regret it, swimming ten strokes out and ten strokes back while the waves broke over him and the rain pelted down or hung fine and chill in the air. Afterwards, he ran up and down the beach, rain washing salt away, his skin lobster-coloured from the cold, and then he put his clothes back on and marched home to the cottage to drink a scalding cup of tea with a dessertspoonful of scotch in it.

—That's better,

he said.

—There's nothing like not being in the sea to make you feel alive.

I myself confined my swimming to clearer days when the waves rolled over and I could lie on my back and float, feeling myself rise and fall. When the weather was fine and there had been no rain to wash the silt out of the river, or any wind to roil the seabed, the water was so clear that you could see the bottom through it, distorted by the ripples to bend and shimmer, and I loved to stand still in it and wait, like the herons did, until things unburied themselves from the sand and scuttled around my feet.

—Look, Grandy!

I shouted.

—A crab!

67

and I watched it run past me, its long legs green and delicate, stepping sideways across the seabed as though onto a stage to dance.

vii

This is how I remember him, when I can – as the man who jogged up and down the beach, who swam, who made jokes and who knew what safety was. Who carried me across his shoulder when necessary, and who seemed to know the workings of everything. I try not to think of him old. I try not to think of him at the high house, sitting in the orchard with a rug folded across his lap, or struggling to climb the stairs. Most of all I try not to think of the last days – how pain shadowed him and I pretended not to understand when he told me what to do.

viii

After I could swim, Grandy taught me to sail. He kept a boat moored in the estuary, a small yacht with a tiny cabin and an engine.

—Can't we just use the motor, Grandy?

I asked, as he tried to explain to me the mysteries of ropes and sheets.

—Where would be the joy in that?

he answered, and he let the wind blow us out across the choppy water where the river butted up against the sea. I never got much good at it, then, although I became better later, out of necessity.

—When I was a boy,

Grandy said,

—there were mackerel shoals so big that they'd be leaping in the boat. You could see them underneath the surface, sometimes. It looked like glitter in the water, some game of light, and the gulls would come, and I'd have enough fish in a few minutes for eating and some left over, and that would be it. Time to turn around, and all the afternoon left over.

Grandy taught me how to cast out the line with its silver lure, how to make it flick and swerve through the water to mimic the sprats and sand eels which the mackerel chased. After an hour, perhaps, we might have a few fish, small ones, and Grandy would say that it would do, and he would turn the boat for home while I, exhausted, wind-blasted, lay on the narrow deck and watched the sea run past. I liked the taste of the fish. I liked it more than the crabs we caught in pots, which I couldn't help but think of as they had been when in motion, running away from me across the sand.

ix

In winter, we wrapped ourselves in layers, T-shirts and jumpers with waterproofs on top, and we went out as usual, Grandy because he had work to do and me because I was yet to realise that I had the choice. Grandy had a wax coat that came down to his ankles, and under it he wore thick-soled boots and gaiters, two pairs of trousers, jumpers layered one above the other. I had snow suits in ascending sizes, until at last I was old enough that Grandy bought me a wax coat of my own, and I was too proud of it to admit how much I missed the cocooning warmth of the suits. There was still work to be done in the gardens, even in winter, and there were roofs which leaked and gutters which clogged, and even if there was nothing pressing Grandy would get out while there was light enough and we would walk together round the edge of the village, out across the heath, through the marshes, over the dunes and along the beach and then back at last up the embankment which held the river to its bed. Often, we would take a bucket with us and as we walked along the beach we would collect periwinkles, cockles, limpets and mussels, these to be purged and cleaned and eaten, flicked from their shells and dipped in mayonnaise, and I am grateful for this knowledge now, because these shellfish are easy food in the winter when we are hungry. They are no effort apart from the collecting, which Pauly and I do together, scrambling over the rocks, picking them out of the pools, pulling aside the seaweed to send the hermit crabs scuttling away and leave the shiny round shells of the winkles exposed, although there are not as many of them as there used to be. Caro doesn't come. She says it is because of her hands, which are prone to cracking and to chilblains and would suffer from the constant dunking into the icy water of the rockpools, but we know that really this is just another way of saying that she is afraid of the sea.

Afterwards, when we had finished our walk and the darkness was setting in, Grandy and I would go back to the cottage to wake up the fire where it smouldered, and we would eat one of Grandy's stews, thick bowls of meat and vegetables spooned over baked potatoes.

—This'll keep the cold off,

Grandy said, and I wonder if the fact that so many of my memories are of food is because it is all we think about, now. Every day in the high house Pauly and Caro and I do nothing but try to make sure that we will have enough to eat so that we might continue to do the same the next day. We must think always about whether the work is worth the reward – food which takes more energy to grow than it can return is worse than a waste. It is a cycle which exhausts us, both the thought of it and the labour, but we don't stop. This, I think, is because of the ways we are tied together, and I wonder if this is another of those things which Francesca anticipated. Each of us is responsible for the others, and so we can't call an end to it. Besides, the place remains beautiful. There are moments, when I stand on the edge of the water at low tide, when, even though my hands are numb from their dousing in cold water, I watch the silver water and the pink-grey winter sky, when the oystercatchers and the redshanks and the curlews pick their way around me, that my heart leaps at the sight of it – and there are moments when I lift potatoes and am filled with satisfaction, the way we waste nothing that might be useful, turning the earth and digging it through with the compost which we have made. These are the moments that we cling to, that we husband as carefully as we do everything else, so they might keep us going.

x

Did Grandy teach me these things because he anticipated what was to come? This is what I think I should have asked him, when I had the chance – but I think that, had I done so, he would have said it was only how we lived. What guiding principle was ever needed, besides habit, and the peculiar happiness of home?

xi

—Maisie's mum has a fridge which makes ice cubes when you press a button,

I told Grandy.

—And they have a television and when you tell it what you want to watch, it starts your programme for you. Maisie does it all the time. And Emma has her own laptop in her bedroom. We don't even have a computer.

He looked at me.

—Do you know what is meant by 'anachronism'?

he asked.

—Yes. I read it in a book. Are you talking about us, or the fridge?

Grandy laughed.

—Ah, well,

he said,

—time for tea.

xii

I did my homework at school when I needed a computer for it. The teachers let me stay. Or I went to the library, and waited for Grandy there, when I was still at the primary and he had to come and pick me up in the elderly Volvo he still kept, then. The village school had closed decades before. Later, when I went on to the big comprehensive on the hill above the town, a bus came for me in the morning, and in the afternoon it brought me home again, and Grandy got rid of the car.

—Not worth the petrol,

he said, as he waved goodbye to its new owner, who had come to drive it away.

Our village was the last stop on the bus route and I the only child who lived there, and every day the driver asked me if I minded getting out at the junction with the main road instead of further down because the road through the village ran to the dunes and then stopped, the whole village one huge dead end, and there was barely room to turn the bus around. I said I didn't mind at all, and walked the last mile across the heath, scaring up pheasants as I went. When I reached the village, on the way to Grandy's cottage, I passed the old schoolhouse. It was a holiday let, now, and in its garden, underneath a square trellis across which Grandy had trained a honeysuckle and clematis, there was a hot tub.

xiii

On winter evenings, Grandy read to me, while I sat and drew, or built things out of Lego.

—Look, Grandy,

I said, holding up what I had made,

—a unicorn—

And then, a little later,

73

—A family of unicorns.

I used to do the same to Pauly, through the long nights in the winter when we stoked up the kitchen stove and stayed in that one warm room as long as we could. I made charcoal sticks on the fire and let Pauly draw with them on the slate floor, making a game out of washing it off, or he would build with Lego in his turn, my old stuff fetched from the attic in Grandy's cottage the summer Pauly came to the high house, and the new sets Francesca had bought for him and stored in the barn, the whole lot now muddled together and kept under the sofa in a red suitcase. In the room which Francesca had prepared for Pauly, the year before he and Caro came, there was a bookcase, its shelves stacked with children's books, all new when Pauly first arrived, their spines uncracked, and on those dark evenings when we eked out the power stored in the generator to run the lights, or used one of our store of wind-up torches, Caro and I took it in turns to read. When Pauly was older, we taught him to play cards, and Caro tried to teach him chess – and on her good days, her joyful days, when she came back from a run along the river light and free and full of energy, they played hide-and-seek together, dashing about the unlit rooms to hide while I, exasperated, excluded, followed behind them, shutting the doors to keep the heat in.

xiv

When Grandy was a boy, he told me, our village had been only one of a string which ran along the coast like beads on a neck-lace, and each one was its own, particular and distinct – each

one had its pub, its post office, its school; each one had its
fishing boats and farms – but by the time I was born the
others were as hollow as ours was. There were still the farms,
but they were no longer worked by people who came up from
the village. Machines did the harvest labour and the owners of
them scraped by, one season to the next, at the mercy of wet
autumns, late springs – or they were owned by corporations,
companies with their offices in a distant city. The harbour
was empty except for Grandy's yacht and a few others like it,
kept for pleasure, and the bright red open boats which took
tourists out in summer to look for seals.

—Where do people think their food comes from?

Grandy asked, as we listened to a woman on the radio
complain about the price of bread.

—Do they think it arrives in a pod?

xv

In summer, the emptiness of the village was barely noticeable.
Then the green was busy with the people who had bought the
houses, or who had rented them, come for their holidays. The
people who came regularly all seemed to know one another.
They organised entertainments in the church hall, where
in the winter, when I was small, I used to put on plays for
Grandy, performing all the parts on the scuffed stage. There
were sports days and fancy-dress competitions. The children
ran about in gangs, on the green where the swings were or
down by the beach, sharing ice creams and jokes, the younger
ones with buckets and spades and the older ones sitting on

the dunes, tangled in close knots, legs and arms draped over one another. I never learned any of their names. They smiled at me when I passed, but I wasn't invited to join and was too proud to ask. On warm evenings with the sun slanting golden on the green and the swallows swerving through the air the village seemed a paradise, with everyone in it healthy and happy, and all the front doors freshly painted, and all the gardens filled with flowers.

—Such a wonderful community,

I heard a man say one afternoon in July as he queued up to buy a postcard.

—Perhaps,

the woman with him said,

—but have you seen how much the houses cost? And you couldn't live here full-time. Imagine the winter, and having to drive miles every time you needed a pint of milk—

It was the same at Christmas, when the lights were strung from house to house. On Christmas Eve they all stood round the big tree on the green, drinking mulled wine and singing carols, but by Twelfth Night they were gone again. That was when the bad weather set in, often, after the crisp deep-winter days when the frost illuminated the earth and everything – sea, sky, river – shone pale in the light from the low-hanging sun. That was the old year's last glory, before the new one slunk over the threshold bringing the grey months, when rain blew loud against windows, or fog shrouded everything in its damp folds, and the sea was hard and inhospitable, beating itself against the sand, bringing seaweed up the beach in heaps to rot and stink. Then the river bled across the marshes where it could, or chafed at the cuts made to hold it back, and wherever I went I could feel the water, waiting. At half past five on a January afternoon it was obvious how the village had been emptied. The houses were shut up. Their windows were blank, and when the dark began to spread in across the sea you could feel the chill coming off them, their curtains open onto cold rooms, their chimneys smokeless – but love for something broken can be so much easier to feel than love for something whole. Look at Pauly's love for Caro, the way he watches her, the way he is so careful with her. Me too, I suppose. I mean, I am careful with her. I tell her to eat, to rest, to put an extra layer on and remember to wear her gloves, and on her good days I feel a glow of pride to see that she is happy.

xvi

This was the result of it all: that for nine and a half months of the year the village was ours, mine and Grandy's, and when I remember it this way – when I remember the empty days which rolled like the waves from sunrise to sunset, the sea and the sky close and the two of us between them – then it seems that even in the worst of winter it must have been a paradise which stretched until the fall.

xvii

In summer, on fine evenings, I did my homework on the garden bench, my legs crossed and my exercise books thrown down beside me, while Grandy came and went, pottering about the garden, lifting leaves, inspecting earth, his secateurs and trowel in the pockets of his garden waistcoat, and then when I was finished he would come and sit next to me, our legs stretched out in front of us, his long, mine shorter but still growing. Sometimes Grandy drank a glass of his home-brewed cider, or we both drank tea. In front of the bench the lawn sloped down towards the herb patch, and beyond that the vegetable beds, the bean rows and the bright yellow flowers of the Jerusalem artichokes, the bushy courgettes, the potato plants, the fruit cage with its rows of raspberries, summer and autumn, trained to stakes, the gooseberries and the currant bushes – and, beyond again, the stone boundary wall in which a wild rose had rooted, and on the other side of it the village, its pantiled roofs a jumble between the river and the sea. Often, we sat in silence, or we talked about nothing in particular – the details of our days, the trivia of house and garden. We liked to watch the light fade as the sun fell behind us, picking out the branches of the trees in gold, and we liked to watch the swallows wheel and swoop, diving to catch the insects which hummed above the water channels – until, one year, they didn't come. May turned to June, June to July, and Grandy and I waited, but the sky was empty, except for the gulls which kept on turning slowly, high above, reflecting the setting sun from their white bellies back down to us.

—Perhaps they're only late,

I said, and then,

—perhaps this year they've gone somewhere else.

Grandy shrugged. I said,

—I'm sure they'll come back.

—Of course,

he said,

—of course they will—

but there was no sign of them that year, or the next, and I am still waiting, now. I watch for them each spring, from the kitchen window in the high house. I stand there in the early evening, when the light begins to fade, when the insects rise, still not so numerous, into the dimming air, and I wish for them, for their bullet bodies and the way they have of flickering in flight, their speed and grace – but the sky is still empty. Perhaps there are no swallows left.

xviii

There were more absences, after that, or we began to notice those which had already happened. There was a muting of the insect hum, and bees were found dying in drifts at the base of the trees they had their hives in. We missed the bats which used to streak out from the church at dusk. An oak tree which grew on the heath, its trunk so thick I couldn't get my arms around it, put out no leaves in spring, and in autumn a high wind blew it to the ground.

xix

When I started secondary school, Grandy bought me a laptop.

—You'll be needing it for homework,

he said, and at the sight of the computer's slim silver

casing on the kitchen table I threw my arms around his neck in gratitude – and then, gratitude done, I turned the laptop on. The internet connection in the village was very good, because of all the summer visitors who needed it for work, and now it became my other world, after Grandy was in bed. My computer was a link to what was beyond the village, beyond the town – beyond the library which wouldn't lend me all the books I wanted to read because I wasn't old enough, and the school where I was looked at sideways for all the things I didn't know, and most of the things that I did. Late at night, scrolling through news sites, I read about those things which were beginning to happen elsewhere. That winter, in the southern hemisphere, a forest fire encroached on a city and whole suburbs were burned to the ground. I watched people running from their houses. I watched them coughing in a pall of smoke. I watched them line up on a beach, everything behind them burning, and wait to be rescued. They got into the sea and stood, waist-deep in water, waiting, because there was nowhere left for them to run.

—We have lost everything,

a man said, standing on the deck of the navy ship which had come to rescue them,

—and what will be done to help us?

His face was grimed with soot, and one of his hands rested on the head of a child who stood, silent, watchful, at his hip. After that, I watched an earthquake, and then it was an outbreak of cholera, a flood, a drought. Each time the questions were the same. Each time, people gave money, for a while, and then there was something else, and the last thing was forgotten by all except those who, presumably, still lived inside of it. To watch became a hobby or a habit, and I thought I was better for it, because at least I knew what was going on – but what difference did my knowledge make? Outside, in the garden, things went on. The owls hooted. A fox barked. In the morning, I ate my porridge and got dressed for school. We were no better than anyone else, Grandy and I. We noticed the changes, but we dismissed them, or said that they were only a part of the inevitable, because doesn't the world always change, one way or another? Loss was familiar to us. The village had always been beleaguered and so, when we saw the dunes erode, when the marshes flooded a month earlier than usual and the reeds cracked dry in the summer from drought – when Grandy, in his small boat on fine days, caught strange fish or nothing at all – when three dead dolphins in a month washed up on the beach and rotted – we shook our heads, and we were sad, but we dismissed it as just the sort of thing that happens, so close to the sea. We reported the dolphins to the coastguard and, having done our duty, forgot about them.

xx

Years later, on one of those strange days directly after the storm, when I felt that I was still waiting for something but didn't yet know what it was, I sat next to Grandy in his room in the high house. He was too ill, then, to move further than the chair by the window which I helped him into each morning, pulling another next to it so that we could be side by side, our hands resting on our knees. Together, we looked out across the orchard, the bare branches of the apple trees twisting against the sky, the clipped hedge a sharp line at its back.

—Let it grow,

Grandy had said about the grass when we first came to the high house.

—Mowing it's a waste of energy. There's a scythe in the barn. Use that twice a year. The trees are old enough to cope with the competition—

and so it had become a sort of meadow, winter grass gone over to seed, and flattened by six weeks or more of inundation, but beyond the flattening, no sign of devastation – only, now that it had stopped, the aftermath of heavy rain, the smell of wet earth and the sound of water, dripping. We watched Pauly, in his waterproof dungarees and bright blue coat, zigzag his way through the trees, intent on his own business.

—I've been to look,

I said.

—The village is under water.

Grandy kept looking straight ahead, at Pauly. I didn't know if I was waiting for him to speak. At last, he said,

—It'll go down. But not by much. I expect the river will be there for good, now. You couldn't put it back. Not without rebuilding all the banks, and even then—

Pauly had something in his hand. Seeing us at the window he held it out, his fingers cupped around his palm, but he was too far away and we couldn't see what it was.

—The phone lines are down,

I said.

82

—And the internet is patchy. Half the country is under water, as far as I can tell. The Thames has burst its banks above the barrier and god knows how many people drowned. They say it's worse in the Netherlands – Belgium and Germany, too. Switzerland has closed its borders. The French government say that they have suffered their own damages and don't have the resources to send aid. People have nowhere to go. Some of them were sitting on roofs, making videos of the water rising. Some of them were waiting to die. Grandy—

but I didn't know how to say what I was thinking. All morning, between the rising spirits brought on by our own escape and the sudden blue skies, an end to rain after weeks of storms, a sense of desolation had come over me in waves.

—We should have done something,

I said,

—we should have tried—

—Tried what?

asked Grandy, and I knew that he was right, but still it didn't rinse us clean from blame.

xxi

Things happen slowly, and then all at once. I don't remember Grandy getting old, but by the time I was in my mid-teens he had stopped swimming every day. He was wary on ladders. He carried a stick. Often, in the garden, kneeling to weed between cabbages, he would pause before standing up and then do so slowly, in stages, his hands on the ground, then on his knees, and then at last he would huff himself upright.

I noticed these things when I wasn't looking for them – when I caught sight of him through a window, or coming unexpectedly round the bend in the lane, or when I saw him in the churchyard, resting on an upright gravestone. Then I noticed how white his hair had become, and how his body seemed to have grown strangely proportioned, his arms lengthened and his back shortened, his legs bowed, and I realised how long it had been since I saw him run – but isn't this how change always becomes visible? After years of incremental alteration you stand, surrounded by your accommodations, and wonder for the first time at the fact that everything should, somehow, have come to this.

xxii

The night before I left for my first term at university, Grandy cooked the fish he had caught that afternoon, fresh mackerel with bottled rhubarb. He made fried potatoes. We ate in the garden, at the trestle table which I had pulled out from the shed. Grandy had been to town on the bus that afternoon and come back with a bottle of wine.

—The real stuff,

he said, as he showed it to me.

—No more of my hedgerow filth for you.

He poured a glass for me then one for himself, which he raised in my direction.

—Your health,

he said.

—I'm proud of you, Sal—

Then, later, sighing,

—I wish that I had gone. But things were different then. What I know I taught myself, and I don't think I've made a bad job of it, all told. But still—

It had not occurred to me before that Grandy's life might seem, either to himself or to someone else, to be a disappointment. I had never thought that he might have wanted something other than he had. I had assumed he was happy, and had never thought to ask if it were true.

—Of course,

I said,

—not a bad job at all,

but my words sounded false, as though I were lying, and I was angry with myself for saying them.

xxiii

I studied history, and I enjoyed it – I enjoyed the work and, after the village, the fact of being surrounded by people, the ability to make friends easily, to visit people on a whim – but I missed Grandy, although not so much that, when Christmas came and I was invited to go and stay in a cottage in the New Forest with some people on my course, I didn't take the chance. I asked Grandy for the money and he gave it, although where it came from I don't know – his savings, I suppose, because later, when the roof began to leak, we had to put buckets under the drips and hope it didn't get worse.

All the time I was away, for the first term, and then the holidays, and then the second term, he wrote me letters, one a week, across pages of lined A4 paper, folded up neatly into thirds and posted with a second-class stamp. The postbox in the village was only emptied weekly in winter, although it was daily in summer because of all the postcards people sent – and often, I think, between January and May, Grandy's letter must have been the only thing that was inside it. In his letters he told me about the garden and the sea, the birds that he had counted, the trips he had made by bus to town to do his shopping, and who he had seen while he was there. *I met your primary teacher, Mrs Baker, while I was getting library books,* he wrote. *She said to tell you that she is very proud of you.* His handwriting was slanting, cursive, old-fashioned and hard to decipher, and I had to read his letters slowly, sitting in a good light. I still have them. I keep them in the biscuit tin which used to be in Grandy's pantry and is now at the bottom of the wardrobe in my bedroom at the high house, but I don't take them out often because I am afraid that, if I read them too many times, then they will lose their power of invocation, the ability they have to bring him, or something of him, into a room. When I do, though, what I see in them is what I missed at the time, or chose to ignore – his pride in me and his determination to let me have my run at things, but also his anxiety, the fear that all around him change was coming fast and unfettered, the seasons falling into one another, the delicate systems he had spent his life observing starting to unravel. *I walked along the dunes today,* he wrote, *and I see that in many places the grass is thin, and even, in some areas, entirely worn away. The tides are getting higher. Since the new year I have waited for floods, but we have been lucky so far. How do your essays go? The*

*new season's garlic is starting to sprout, which is a little before
expected and I am afraid that with this mild weather, and so
much rain, at least half of it will rot. Walking back from looking
over the garden at the schoolhouse I saw a badger in the lane,
a fine chap, but awake too early, I think. I bought some tins of
cat food in the town last week and have been leaving it out for
him. At Easter we must take the boat out. It has been months
since I caught a fish* – and in the margin, in ink, a picture of
the badger, its nose snuffling along the lines on the paper.
Underneath, Grandy has written, again, *A fine chap* – and,
sitting on the side of my bed in the high house, I rub my finger
across the letters, along the badger's cross-hatched back, its
stripes, its claws, as though in doing so I might touch the hand
which drew them.

xxiv

I wrote back, but not as often as once a week, and my letters,
in contrast to Grandy's, were short. I would like to be able to
say that I wasn't thoughtless – but it would be, at best, a half-
truth. I missed Grandy but I was busy, and when I wrote it was
about parties and essay crises, about friends and the friends of
friends, play rehearsals, clubs, about the college library which
was open all night and how, once, I had fallen asleep on a sofa
there and not woken up until morning. When I had written
what seemed to me to be enough, I scrawled my name at the
bottom, stuffed the page into an envelope, and felt my guilt
ease off. It wasn't calculated to hurt, but he felt so far away.
How could I explain to him the mixture of excitement and

fear I felt, because I enjoyed what I was doing, and worked harder than I let on, but still couldn't see anything of myself in it? There was no trace in the texts that I was set of Grandy, or of what he had been at pains to teach to me – the village's long, quiet span – the ways that it had bent and crept along, without the means to grow beyond itself, but neither, ever, quite disappearing. I found no mention of the idea that such a small survival might be, in itself, enough – a way to live which was not notable, which did not aspire but did not, either, take more than it put back, nor push off the cost of enterprise else-where, outsourcing, as we so often did, our suffering. Once, in a seminar, I tried to explain, but I found that, as I did so, Grandy became someone else – more admirable, but less himself, and so I stuttered into silence and then, embarrassed, excused myself, and left the room.

xxv

I'm not sure that I'll have time for the boat, I wrote to Grandy, *because I will have a lot of work to do getting ready for my exams* – but as the end of the spring term approached, I counted down the days. I packed my rucksack. I locked my bedroom door. I got on the train, and as it rattled towards the coast, as the towns became villages and grew farther apart, as the fields became familiar, I felt my heart lift. I stood up and went into the space between the carriages so that I could see better. I opened the window to feel the fresh air, and when I saw the station coming I leaned forward, as though by doing so I could make the train go faster, and when it reached the platform and stopped I fiddled impatiently with the door until the catch released. I went out through the station and took the bus to the village and there was Grandy, stood at the bus stop waiting for me, his hands in his pockets, his old brown hat on his head, and I hurried towards him with my bag slung over my shoulder because I loved him and I had missed him – but, as we walked side by side down the lane and Grandy asked me about my term, I found that the voice I used to speak to him was the voice of my letters.

We got to the cottage and it was exactly how it had always been, except that it seemed smaller, and colder, and it felt blank, as though it were hiding something from me. I realised that Grandy had tidied, and I felt a twisting in my stomach. I went upstairs to my room and unpacked my rucksack, putting my university library books on the shelf next to my dog-eared copy of *The Lion, the Witch and the Wardrobe*, and then it was dinner time, and I went down to the kitchen, which was as warm as ever and smelled of cooking. I kissed Grandy on the cheek and felt much better, except that I couldn't help but notice the jar of Bisto granules, or how the pepper in the pepper pot had been pre-ground.

xxvi

I stayed for a month, the length of the holiday, and summer came while I was there, and with it the people who owned the houses. I heard their voices in the lane, and when I went down to the beach I saw them, their feet thudding back and forth across the marram grass – and Grandy was right, it did seem thinner than it had been before, worn away completely in places so that the sand beneath it spilled out, leaving deep gouges in the dunes. I didn't go out often. I spent most of the time in my room, working. I didn't go out on the boat. Grandy brought me cups of tea, and I waited for him to tell me that I worked too hard, but he said nothing, and then the holiday was over, and I stood at the bus stop, my backpack at my feet, and was relieved at being let out of something that was so complicated.

xxvii

After the Easter holidays I began to go, two or three times a week, to the meetings of the ecological societies and climate activist groups which were held regularly in the student common room. I sat at the back and listened while, one after another, earnest speakers described the environmental impact of this or that plastic or chemical and action was proposed to force the university to divest from fossil fuels. There were proposals for sit-ins and lecture strikes. There was a feeling of gaiety, of joy at participating. It felt to me like a kind of party, a way people had of bonding themselves together, marking themselves out as a type, and I thought of home. I thought of the beach, and of the shreds of blue plastic which washed in twice daily with the tide and which Grandy and I had always picked up, whenever we walked that way, filling our pockets with them and biting down on the impossibility of ever making a dent in it. I was ashamed to feel so parochial, and ashamed as well to notice, among the chants and the handmade banners painted with vegetable dyes, that although the action itself might have brought a temporary relief from anxiety to those who were a part of it, nothing else changed. The plastics were still manufactured. The chemical fertilisers were still used. The university set up a committee to discuss the possibility of altering its investment patterns but such discussions, we were told, were serious, and, while our points were noted, outcomes would not be determined by blackmail. *I can't tell*, I wrote to Grandy, *which of us is missing the point.*

xxviii

Term ended, and the next day I got up early and took the first train, eager not to waste the day. For weeks I had been thinking of the village, the long days, the light. I had been thinking of swimming and walking, of helping Grandy in the garden, of going out in the boat. I had been thinking of the long tails of the evenings sat on the garden bench, and how, with three months off and no exams to worry about, surely it would be enough time for Grandy and me to settle back into ourselves.

—You'll be wanting out,

Grandy said, after he had welcomed me, watching me carry my bag to the bottom of the stairs.

—A day like this. I made you sandwiches.

I took them gratefully, washed my face and hands, and went out, walking into the bright sunshine with a feeling like my heart opening.

It was early evening before I started back for Grandy's cottage. I had been swimming in the sea, turning and turning in it until for the first time in months I felt clean, and afterwards I walked back along the dunes, tracing the lines of their deterioration. It was hard to tell, coming back like this after a time away, whether things had speeded up – the erosion of place, the unspooling of the pattern of the weather – or whether it was only that, having been away, I saw the changes that had taken place in my absence all at once, without the slow degradation which we barely noticed, day to day. I was tired, both from the swimming and from the effects of the sun, its day-long beat, and my skin felt tight, my body heavy and stretched out. My hair was wet. I smelled of the sea. I came the long way round, skirting the edge of the heath to arrive at Grandy's cottage from above, avoiding the crowds of day trippers and holidaymakers who loitered about the village, dropping their ice creams on the pavements, sitting in the garden of the pub or on the green and shouting to one another as though it were all one big park, a toy place, built for them. I was looking forward to dinner, to lettuce and peas and new potatoes from the garden, and I was expecting Grandy to have made a start on it, so that it was a surprise to me when, pushing open the gate, walking round the side of the cottage, I found him sitting on the garden bench, and with him a woman with long hair.

—Sal!

Grandy called when he saw me,

—Sal, this is Francesca. Francesca – my granddaughter, Sal—

and that was the first time I saw her, and even then I was uncertain, and I didn't know what to say.

Pauly

F ROM the window: pigeons, crows, starlings. In the garden: sparrows.

This is all I can remember of the city. My mother I can't remember at all.

Sally

—I t is a question of preparedness,
Francesca said. It was the end of the first week of the
summer holiday and she was sitting, as she had done every
evening since I came home, on Grandy's garden bench, her
legs stretched out in front of her. She looked, I thought, entirely
ordinary – with her loose white linen vest and navy shorts,
her leather sandals, she might have been any of the women
who came to spend their holidays in the village, except that
I knew who she was because I had seen her on news sites. I had
heard her name in student bedrooms and had read her articles,
her speeches. I had admired her, then, when she seemed the
fierce and angry academic we all thought ourselves capable
of becoming – but now here she was in person, arriving from
nowhere to sit in my place on the bench, and I wasn't sure
I even liked her.

—We can be sure,
she continued,
—that floods will come. There's no doubt on that score.
All we can do is protect what might be saved. It's no good
waiting for the government to intervene, because they won't,
not pre-emptively. I've seen the damage flooding does. The

force of the water is unimaginable. It takes everything it can get.

—But not you,

I muttered, almost under my breath.

i

Since the first evening when I came back to the cottage and found Francesca next to Grandy on the bench, it had seemed as though she was always somewhere nearby. I tried to avoid her, spending my afternoons walking across the dunes or along the river, swimming in the sea – but when I got back from wherever I had been, letting myself through the gate and walking round into the garden, there she would be, waiting.

—Sal!

Grandy would call,

—You're back! I don't suppose you're making tea?

and I would turn and go back to the kitchen, put the kettle on, get out the tray. When I went to fetch the cups down from the shelf, my hand hovered over the third, undecided every time – but however much I might want to, for the look of it, to make a point, I still couldn't bring myself to leave Grandy and Francesca by themselves in the garden, and so I took the three cups and added them to the tray, carried it outside, sat down where I could listen. It seemed to me, then, that Grandy had found in Francesca something he had failed to find in me. He talked to her – reflectively, seriously – as an equal, and as he did so she sat, cup cradled in both hands, listening. He told her about himself and about the village, about the ways it had been beleaguered and, always, about his love for it. It didn't occur to me until much later that what I was watching, angrily, from my place on the lawn might constitute an interview of sorts – of Grandy by Francesca, and the other way about. I didn't wonder whether Francesca might have sought Grandy out, or what they might want from one another. I saw only how she had come and taken the space which had been mine. For the best part of a year I had left Grandy behind, and now I found that he had not waited.

ii

One morning, while Grandy stood at the cooker stirring a pan of porridge for our breakfast, I said,

—What's Francesca even doing here?

Grandy shrugged.

—She's staying at the high house. She's restoring it. It's good it's getting used again.

—That's not what I meant,

I said.

—I meant, what's she doing here, with us? She's always hanging about. What does she want?

Grandy raised his eyebrows, but gave no other answer. I ate my porridge and went out straight away, walking up along the river to the heath, where I stayed, sulking, until hunger drove me home again.

iii

I had spent all day in the sun. My feet hurt from walking across shingle and I was thirsty. I came through the gate. Francesca was in her habitual spot on the bench, and Grandy was further down the garden, picking runner beans. He saw me, waved, held a handful of beans in the air.

—For Francesca,

he called – then, seeing my expression, or guessing at it, said,

—Well, we have so many.

—I offered to help him pick them,

Francesca added,

—but he wouldn't let me.

I shrugged.

—Don't you have a son somewhere?

I asked, and turned away before she had time to answer.

iv

Perhaps there were evenings when Francesca wasn't there, when it was just Grandy and me. Or perhaps there were times when the two of them spoke of something other than Grandy's life, and the village – but if so, I don't remember them. What I remember is how I sat on the grass with a book open in front of me, pretending to read, and how quiet it was, apart from their voices. I think that I hated myself and Francesca equally, then – myself, because I was unable to stop listening, because I couldn't be gracious but could only sit, noisily turning the pages of my book; and Francesca, because she asked those questions which it had never occurred to me to ask, and Grandy answered them.

—You must remember the last big flood,

Francesca said.

—How old would you have been? Seven? Eight?

—Something like that,

Grandy said.

—We thought at the time it would be the end of us, but the water went down in the end. The river went back to its bed.

ν

For days, Francesca pushed Grandy to talk about the last time the village had flooded, but he would not be drawn, and I was glad, because although I had learned about it at school, sitting in a dark classroom watching black-and-white videos of flooded fields, dead cows turning and turning in the currents, or of roofs like flotillas where villages had been, their inhabitants crouching at the edges of the water, it had never occurred to me that Grandy might be somewhere among them. Our own history and that of the classroom always seemed so far apart – and I was ashamed, because I saw now how I had lacked both curiosity and imagination. Grandy seemed, all at once, to be apart from me, and, because of that, to be very precious.

—I can't tell you anything you won't know already,

he said to Francesca, and instead he talked about the garden, and about the landscape, the way it had been formed by water and by the pacification of water, the attempts to keep the sea at bay, and how for years at a time the tide would stay where it was put, and the people who lived along the edge of it would think that they had won out, this time – until the next storm, the next flood, the next scourging.

vi

Three centuries ago, Grandy said, the shape of the whole area of land around the village had been different. The river hadn't made its estuary through the small harbour in our village, but instead, just beyond the current tideline, had turned south, cut off from the sea by a spit of land, mainly shingle, which had run to the east of it, perhaps a mile out from the current coastline. The river continued south for a further seven miles or so, until at last the shingle petered out and gave the river its mouth. A port was built around it, the slowness and width of the river creating a peculiarly safe and sizeable harbour, used both for fishing and for trade. The spit itself was substantial enough that it had a strip of marram grass growing the whole length of it, the matted roots holding sand and stones in place, stabilising it, so that while still less than land, it was more than sandbank. In the summer, at least, it was inhabited both by many birds – by plovers and egrets, oystercatchers, lapwings, terns – and by the fishermen who used the grass for nets, and for the roofs of the shiels which they had built there to save themselves the trouble of going home. On those fine, short nights in the middle of the year it must have been a glory, Grandy said, to lie with water on either side and the half-dark sky above. He said he believed that people have always been called by such places. Perhaps, he went on, we want to feel the pull of nothing, how easily we might slip towards it, the same way we stand and stare upwards at the vaulted roof of a church and can feel god calling. An emptiness that asks to be filled.

Francesca listened, and I watched her watching him, her face turned to Grandy's while his was turned away, towards the open sky, blue and wide above the garden wall. I expected to see something mocking there – a trace of contempt, perhaps, for an old man and his stories – but instead she looked quite gentle, as though Grandy's words had moved her, and it made me even angrier, to see this softness in her, because it was not what I had wanted, which was to find a justification for my dislike.

vii

Aside from its use as a source of grass, Grandy said, and as a place for the men to wait in summer while their nets, strung across the river, filled up with fish, for the duration of its existence this narrow strip protected the area on its landward side from the full force of both tide and weather – and so, he said, the town which centred on the port was both prosperous and stable. Its boundaries spread wide, down from the rise of the cliffs and onto the low-lying riverbank itself – and, looking from their windows, people must have seen the river's far side, the bulk of the shingle blocking out the sea, and thought themselves protected. They built churches and guilds. They built wharfs. They were ambitious. Charters were granted and fortunes made – and the end, when it came, was abrupt, and absolute. Of course, it was possible that, beneath the low-water mark, a slow erosion of the spit had been carrying on, unseen, for almost as long as it had existed – and possible, too, that the town's growth, and the use of the shingle spit as an increasingly permanent settlement, had partly contributed to its destabilisation. Or perhaps it was only one of those things that happen, on the coast, periodically, when people forget how precarious things are, so close to the water and with nothing for their living but the sea. Either way, a storm came. Later in the year than might be expected, probably, but otherwise nothing out of the ordinary at first, except that the wind blew from the east and there was a spring tide with it, and a high wind behind a high tide is always something to be wary of. The inhabitants of the town were used to these things, though, and they thought barely enough of it to stay indoors – not, at any rate, until the sea broke through, and by then it was too late. Within an hour, the town was under water.

viii

Another evening, a few days later. Grandy had been talking about the strengths and weaknesses of different potato varieties, but now, at Francesca's prompting, he returned to the subject of the flood. It was not the immediate loss of life which was so devastating, he said to her, while I lay nearby and listened, pulling the petals off the daisies – although the death toll must have been high. It was what came afterwards – because, when the water retreated, it was clear that the mouth of the river had moved. The whole length of the shingle spit had been washed away in the storm. The river flowed straight out into the sea, some six miles north of where it had been before. All those livelihoods which had been built around the river mouth were lost in the course of a single evening, although perhaps it took longer to see the full effect of it, how things could not be put back the way they'd been before. The docks were destroyed, and there was nowhere to rebuild them, even if there'd been the money to do it. The river was gone. The fishing fleet was sunk or wrecked. Ships due to land had to be diverted elsewhere, and merchants found themselves with goods they couldn't reach, or couldn't store, or had no way of moving. In the course of one bad night the whole system, which the day before had seemed inviolable, was brought to collapse.

ix

After the quick end, there came the slow one. The town, much reduced, impoverished, clung on in some form or another, Grandy told us, until he was himself a boy. After the first decimation, its function removed, its edges crumbling into the sea, it continued to shrink, first into a small town, and then into a village, then a hamlet – until, at last, only a few houses remained, and a pub. You would think the people who lived there would have given it up sooner, since it was obvious that the sea wouldn't stop gnawing at the place until there was noth- ing left of it, or at the very least that they would have become resigned to their eventual displacement – but people stayed if they could because it was home, and each new tranche of losses came as a fresh grief for them. Still, Grandy said, it was easy to put off the inevitable as the water encroached by degrees. It was easy to say that there was time – harder to decide, without some precipitating event, that now was the moment to go. Every few years a higher than usual tide would sweep a bit more away, leaving buildings truncated – houses with their back walls split open and their gardens hanging off the edge of the cliff, bindweed clambering over abandoned shrubberies. It was the pub which was the last to fall. Grandy's father took him to watch. Word spread quickly, one wet afternoon just before Christmas, and, despite the bad weather, men up and down the coast put on their waterproofs and walked through the rain to get there. When Grandy and his dad arrived, waves were already breaking just short of the front step and there was still a half hour to go before high tide, but, inside, a fire was lit in the grate, and there were candles on the tables to burn off the midwinter gloom. Someone was singing, and someone else danced, heavy boots drumming a rhythm on the flags. It was a party. Those who had got there soonest were drunk already, and the landlord drunkest of all.

—Come in!

he cried, as Grandy hovered behind his father in the doorway.

—Come in!

When the water began to come under the door they turned and went outside again, two pints apiece, which was everything that was left of the cellar, and they stood, quiet now, in the lee of the stone building while the waves battered against it, casting spray up around them. The rain had stopped, and the party was a wake, the men standing in a line to watch the end come, until, its work done, the tide turned and, one by one, the men began to walk away.

x

Grandy stretched his legs out in from of him.

—It made a difference here, too, of course,

he said,

—although rather in the other direction. We don't like to think it, but most things have their benefit for someone.

Before the river changed course the people in the village had been able to see the sea but they hadn't been able to reach it. To take a boat out they first had to sail downriver to the harbour in the town, and then there were levies to pay, tithes of catches, any other kind of fee or tax that could be thought of, to line the silk pockets of those who were rich enough already – and now, overnight, they found themselves in possession of a harbour of their own. For a while there was a kind of hysteria about it, some sense that the village had been rewarded for just behaviour, a sense almost certainly rooted in guilt, because it would have been obvious what the cost had been. People must have been coming up in dozens from what was left of the town, looking for work, or alms. What they found was little by way of goodwill. A few weeks earlier there had been a thunderstorm, during which lightning had struck the church tower, leaving scorch marks in the vast oak door that couldn't be sanded out of it, and, afterwards, one of the parishioners who happened to have been walking through the churchyard claimed that he had seen the figure of the devil, dressed in black, running south across the heath towards the town. They had brought it on themselves, the man said, and deserved no comfort – and, besides, hadn't the townspeople been taking all they could for years. Now it was the other way about, perhaps, and nothing more than fairness.

xi

—But,

said Francesca,

—even with a harbour this village never expanded?

Grandy stood up, and walked down to the bed where lettuces grew, bending over to pull up the sprinkling of weeds which had sprouted in between the rows. Francesca made as if to help him, but Grandy frowned and shook his head.

A decade after the storm, he told her, just as the village was starting to expand to fit its new prosperity, the entire fishing fleet went out after herring one Tuesday morning in October. The weather, when they left, was clear and still, and the sea was flat, the waves on it hardly more than lapping at the shore. The barometer, which the men kept nailed to a post in the harbour, was dropping, but the village had come to believe in their luck by then and they ignored it, setting out in sunshine, calling to their wives, their children, to one another, boat to boat. An hour later the storm struck, coming like a fit, the sea an animal desperate to shake them off. A number of the boats were swamped immediately, smashed to pieces by the waves.

Of the rest, some tried to run ahead of the storm, and the others turned, racing to make safe home and harbour. The result was the same for both. A few made it back, exhausted. A few turned up, later, sixty miles south. The rest were lost. Two thirds or more of the village men were killed in the space of two hours, Grandy said, while the women and the children stood on the dunes and watched it happen. It was a century before the population recovered, and by that time the world had moved on. Volume had become the cornerstone, and cost. Fish could be got cheaper elsewhere. Other ports had grown to take the slack.

xii

—It's time I was getting back,

Francesca said.

—I have work I need to do before the morning.

Grandy walked her to the garden gate, but before he opened it to let her through he paused, his hand on the latch.

—Of course,

he said,

—it wasn't the end of any world beyond this one. Neither the flood, nor the storm. A few square miles and a handful of people. The same things have happened everywhere, always. But isn't every ending absolute to those who live through it?

Francesca put her hand on his arm, and they stood that way, for a moment, before he opened the gate and let her through, and I wondered what it meant – what other conversations they had had which that gesture alluded to.

xiii

A sudden downpour, the sort of summer storm we were becoming used to. Rain fell in sheets, bashing the earth, flattening plants, and so instead of in the garden we sat at the kitchen table, Grandy, Francesca and I, with the teapot between us. The roof of Grandy's cottage had a leak in it and I could hear the quick tap-tapping of the water hitting the saucepan I had put out to catch the drips. Not long ago, Grandy would have gone up himself to fix the hole, but now he only shrugged when I mentioned it, and reminded me to empty the pan. I thought it was because he was growing too old to climb the ladder, and it might have been that – but I wonder, now, if he didn't already know how soon we would be leaving.

—This isn't going to be like that,

Francesca said.

—There won't be memorials in church halls. No one is going to make up songs. There will be nothing left.

—Nothing?

I asked, and I felt gleeful, as though I had found the point at last, and now could press it home.

—Or only nothing of yours? People have nothing already. People are dying already. How can a threat to you be an apocalypse when the rest of the world is drowning and it's only a fucking preamble?

Francesca stood up.

—Not a preamble. A beginning. And it's too late, now, to make a difference to the outcome. All we can do is choose who we will save.

—And let everyone else go hang?

She smiled at me, a tight little smile.

—Or save no one at all.

xiv

The next afternoon a note came from Francesca, slipped through Grandy's letterbox. It was written on heavy paper and sealed in a cream envelope, both my name and Grandy's written on the front of it.

—Read it out, then,

Grandy said. I looked at the paper, the writing on it clear and fluid, done in real ink.

—She's asking us to tea on Tuesday,

I told him.

—I suppose you'll want us to go.

Until now, I had only ever seen Francesca at Grandy's cottage. I had assumed that she just dropped in each time, as though she had happened to be passing, although it seems more likely that they had made some arrangement between themselves. I had not been expecting any hospitality from her. I had not thought we were on those terms, but Grandy made me write a note back to her, saying that we would come, and I carried it myself to the high house, to the letterbox which was fixed, then, to the wall next to the gate, although one of the first things Pauly did after he came to the high house was to swing on it and pull it off. As I made to lift the letterbox's flap a man appeared, tallish, fairish, thinnish, coming towards me down the path between the orchard and the walled garden.

—Gosh,

he said, smiling at me,

—a letter. For Francesca, I suppose?

I nodded.

—I'm her husband. And you must be Sally? Well, nice to meet you, Sally. Shall I take the letter? It'll save having to fish it out again after you've put it in that bloody box.

I handed it to him and, thanking me, he ambled off again, back up the path, as though he had come to meet me for the sole purpose of carrying the letter.

That was the only time I saw Caro's father, and he seemed a kind man, but there is nothing else that I can think to say about him.

xv

Francesca met us at the gate and walked with us up towards the high house, going slowly so that Grandy should be comfortable. Under one of the apple trees in the orchard a round table was laid for tea. Sandwiches were stacked under a tea towel. A cake was covered with a cloche to keep the flies away. There were three wicker chairs to sit in.

—Of course,

Francesca said, after she had gone to fetch the teapot,

—real self-sufficiency is an impossible goal. It would require so much in terms of skills – and even then, I'm not really sure it can be done, not without some kind of broader community. There is crofting, of course, but that's skills again, and an amount of trade. Anyway, we've done what we can.

After we had drunk our tea, eaten the sandwiches and the cake, we walked back down through the orchard, this time taking the path across the meadow to the tide pool. The sluice gates and mill had been restored, by then. Francesca showed us how they worked, and the small generator that they powered, designed, she said, to last indefinitely without repair.

—Indefinitely?

I asked.

—Its probable lifespan is two hundred years,

Francesca answered, not rising to me,

—according to its designers. Which is hard to test, of course – but then even a half of that counts as indefinite, under the circumstances. Anyway, it will keep the lights on in the winter, a fridge on in the summer.

—For as long as the fridge keeps going,

Grandy said,

—unless it's a magic fridge, too.

Francesca shrugged.

—It will buy time, anyway,

she said.

—For what?

I asked, but she was already moving away, back in the direction of the house.

xvi

After the tide pool, she took us to the vegetable garden, and then the well, the composting toilets, the wash house with its wood-fired boiler which we hardly used, after the first winter, when we decided that grime was inevitable and certainly better than expending the energy necessary to wash. Perhaps even Francesca couldn't imagine how tight the economy might be, between food and effort.

xvii

Last of all, she showed us the barn, the rows and rows of tins lined up on shelves, the boxed-up clothes, the medical supplies, and I wanted to ask again what the point of it all was, but standing in the middle of it – the barn, the pool, the house and its garden – it seemed impossible to form the question. It was all so extraordinary. It was such effort, such labour – and even then I understood, somehow, that it was tied up with love, although I didn't know whose, or for whom.

—I have laid in a supply of morphine,

she said,

—should it be needed.

Grandy nodded.

—Needed for what?

I asked, but they were talking about different varieties of wheat and paid no attention.

xviii

Afterwards, Grandy and I walked slowly home together, back to the cottage.

—She's built herself a fortress,

I said, outrage swelling in my voice. He reached out for my hand, squeezed it—

—I'm not sure it's actually for her, Sal,

he said. And then,

—Try to be a little kind.

—But what did she want to show it to us for,

I asked,

—if not to point out how we will sink, while she stays dry, and watches?

xix

A week or so before the new term began, Grandy and I went to evensong together. Autumn had come. Although the days were still warm, you could feel it in the evening, in the slight chill behind the breeze and the way the sun hung low, casting long shadows across the dry, year's-end grass. Inside the church, the candles were lit. The faces of the wooden angels, high up in the rafters, flickered. There was the smell of dust and stone, and, beyond the plain glass windows, as the service started, dusk had begun its slow closing of doors. A visiting choir waited, shuffling the music in their folders, and then the vicar came. We sat and stood and sat again. I felt, as I always did, a kind of shiver, a movement which was not faith but rather something near to hope – a transcendent smallness, like seeing myself between two mirrors, reduced by the enormity of past and future to nothing more than one term in a series, each iteration listening to the same words in this same place, and each in each autumn thinking of the spring. I said: *I believe in*

God the Father Almighty, Maker of heaven and earth and felt their ghost breaths on my neck. I listened to the Magnificat, the Nunc Dimittis, and then the anthem, winding, knotting, the indifferent singing made perfect by the close association of notes. I turned to Grandy, and saw that he was crying.

Afterwards, as we made our way out of the church and through the churchyard, back towards the village, he said,

—You think that you have time. And then, all at once, you don't.

xx

We didn't take our coats off when we reached the cottage. We sat in the kitchen, which was warm and smelled of the potatoes Grandy had put in the oven to bake before we left for the church. I had put the kettle on to boil, but hadn't made the tea. Grandy said,

—When I was a boy, there was a flood. The whole village under water.

I wanted to prompt him, then, but I found myself thinking of Francesca – of her stillness, and how quietly she had sat, outside on the bench, waiting for him to be ready to speak – and perhaps that was the first time I felt some gratitude towards her, because, at last, into the silence between us, he carried on.

xxi

The weather had been bad for weeks, he told me, wet and blowy day after day. His father, he said, was a fisherman, as

I knew, and he was away, stuck up the coast waiting for the wind to turn so that his boat could make it back, and so it was only Grandy and his mother at home, and his sister, who was not much more than a baby. They ate their tea, listened to *Children's Hour* on the radio. A woman who lived a few doors down dropped in to say that her brother had just come back from town and it seemed that a river further north had burst its banks – but it was only gossip. The rivers were always spreading somewhere, when the winters were wet. It gave you a little thrill to think about it, a sharp thrum of fear, and then the relief that while others might be wet, you yourself were dry.

After the neighbour had gone, they ate their tea and went to bed, and Grandy slept for a few hours, until the sound of splashing woke him. He put his dressing gown on, and his slippers, and went downstairs to find his mother stood, the baby on her hip, mopping with bath towels at the water which had started to run in under their front door, and he could hardly bear to think of it even now, he said – the sight of his mother in her winceyette nightgown with his father's gaiters underneath it, trying to keep the sea out with a bath mat.

There was a banging on the door and when they opened it, they were met with a surge of water and another of their neighbours, a retired fisherman who knew that Grandy's dad was away.

—Come on now,

he said,

—come on, love, we'd best be going.

Grandy's mother tried to go back to fetch coats for the children but he wouldn't let her.

—There isn't time,

he said, and took both her arms to stay her, so Grandy was in nothing but his pyjamas and his dressing gown as they ran, he and his mother holding hands, his sister slung over the neighbour's shoulder. They were making for the church, and the water was already up to Grandy's knees when they started. The darkness was so thick it was like blindness, and although the neighbour had a torch, it lit up only rain and the water in front of them, which was already changing the shape of things, confusing a familiar landscape as thick snow might, smoothing it or stretching it, but the church bell was ringing, tolling the alarm, and so they navigated by that, keeping it, as far as they could, in front of them. What should have been a five-minute walk took them, running, half an hour, and more than once during that time Grandy lost his footing, tripping and feeling the water start to pull him sideways – but somehow, each time, he managed to catch hold of something, a wall or a gate, and get himself back on his feet.

By the time they reached the turning up to the church the water was past his waist and if, he said, they had left it any later – if his mother had got her way and gone back for their coats – then perhaps they, too, would have been among the ones who drowned.

xxii

It was weeks before they could get back into the house, and, when they did, they found that it was full of sand and silt, and all the furniture was swollen with water and starting to rot. Salt had got into the walls. It was in the plaster and it couldn't be got out, spreading each autumn through any amount of paint or paper. Grandy said that every time they thought they'd seen the last of it, back it would come, creeping out when the wet weather started, to remind them where the water had been – and memory, he said, was no different to the salt. The woman who had come the afternoon before the flood to see his mother, who had sat at their kitchen table talking about the weather, had been woken by the same man who banged on the door of Grandy's house, but while they had left at once, she had stayed behind to try and move her best china plates upstairs and out of danger. A few days afterwards, Grandy told me, his face turned towards the window whose curtains we had not yet drawn, although it was dark enough, now, to do so – a few days afterwards he had been out walking, along the edge of the fields, across which floodwater lay in sheets, and there she was, their neighbour, caught in a hedge, heels up and completely naked, the clothes having been stripped from her body by the water in which she had drowned. He didn't know what to do, he said, because it seemed wrong to tell anyone that he had seen her that way, her skin so pale and splitting, but he couldn't just leave her, either. In the end he wrote a note and posted it through the front door of his schoolteacher's house, and then he went home, and hid in his room, and wouldn't come out until he was sure in his mind that they would have found the woman's body, and got it out of the hedge.

xxiii

—I am afraid, though,

   Grandy said,

   —that Francesca is right. Next time it will not be the same. The sea is rising. The dunes are shrinking. When the next big flood comes, it won't go down again. We were left with less than we had, last time, but it was not nothing, and there were other places to go for anyone lucky enough – but I think that when next time comes there will be no coming back, and not much leaving, either. What will you do, Sal?

   —We,

   I said,

   —what will we do—

   Grandy stood up, and went to get the potatoes out of the oven.

xxiv

One last conversation, the night before I went away – I had been packing my things into my bag but had come down, now, to the kitchen, to make a ham sandwich, which I ate standing at the counter so that the crumbs fell into the sink. Earlier in the day, Grandy had taken the bus to town to visit the library, and he had come home with a selection of newspapers, which he sat reading behind me at the table, grunting occasionally in agreement or derision. It was a companionable way to be, him with his paper, me eating my sandwich and thinking of nothing in particular, and we stayed as we were until, at last,

I heard Grandy shake out his paper and fold it up. I turned
to look at him.

—My father,

he said,

—once met the man who had been navigator to the last
commercial sailing vessel left running the clipper route. He'd
taken her round the Horn, he said, six times or seven, before
she was finally decommissioned. Dad told me it was like
speaking to a ghost. Not just because of how old he was, but
because he seemed to be left over from a world that no longer
existed. A relic. He hadn't moved on, you know. He told dad
that it seemed awful to him, how much he had watched being
forgotten – all the arts and crafts of wooden ships, he said, and
then the rest of it, the manned lighthouses, sextants, celestial
navigation. All gone. It took him years to learn it, only for it to
become obsolete. Dad told me that he had seemed, the man,
as though he needed to tell someone, just so that he could be
sure that the loss at least would be remembered.

Grandy sighed.

—I don't know what to think about Francesca,

he said.

—She is right that what might come now will not be like
what has gone before, but I am an old man, and I have seen
worlds end myself. I have seen the end of this village, for a start.

—It's not ended,

I said.

—We still live here.

—Changed, then,

Grandy said.

—I have seen it changed past recognition.

—Francesca thinks,

I said,

—that what is different is that this time there will be no afterwards.

Grandy snorted.

—If she thinks that, then what's she doing at the high house? She knows there'll be something left. A ruined living, maybe, and a hard world, but hasn't it always been that way for most? All I can think is that what's different now is that no one can claim this is progress.

Later, Grandy came upstairs, where I was packing the last of my books into the top of my rucksack. Only my laptop was left, smooth-cornered and incongruous on the battered wood of the desk. Grandy stood in the doorway, watching me.

—I'll miss you,

he said, and I turned and hugged him, then, the first time I had done so in years, because we were not tactile people and hadn't regularly touched since I had been a small child – but I am glad, now, that we did, because the memory of it, alone of all my memories of that summer, is uncomplicated, and is a joy.

Pauly

M EMORY begins, in snatches, with the journey. There was the rattle of the train, and the birds seen through the window – an egret in a river, pheasants in a field; and then the gulls, hovering above a combine harvester. I remember my hands' span against the glass, its cool against my forehead. Caro, unwrapping sandwiches. The slow emptying, station by station, of the carriage, until there was only Caro and me, and one other woman who watched us, her face frowning – and then it was just the two of us, and when the train ran to a halt at the buffers at the end of the line there was no one to get out onto the single platform but ourselves. We stood, blinking in the sunshine, smelling earth and pigs. Behind us, the train hissed and settled. Its doors closed. I heard a lark, but couldn't see it.

Sally

THE new term began, and I fell back into it. Within days, I had largely forgotten about the things which had preoccupied me over the summer, and if I thought about Francesca at all it was with little more than a pang of shame at having behaved badly – and so it was a surprise, one afternoon, to be called out of a lecture and into the administration office, and to be handed a phone, through which her voice came. I sat on a swivel chair in front of someone else's computer and let it swing gently side to side. Francesca told me that she had found Grandy that morning, lying on the grass in front of the old schoolhouse. She spoke calmly and directly, as though it were a lesson she was giving me. It seemed that he had fallen while trying to clear the gutter above the porch, and it was quite by chance she had found him. He had been lying there since the previous evening, and, although it had been a warm night, he was suffering from exposure, and his hip was broken. She said that she would come and get me, straight away, in her car, and drive me to the hospital. I needn't worry, she said, matter-of-factly. Grandy was in no immediate danger. But there were things I would need to think about. She would tell me on the journey – and I thanked her, wondering, as I put the phone down and went back to my room to pack my bag, how I should have come, all at once, to find her kind.

i

We drove east, slowly shedding the company of other cars, turning into smaller roads, running out towards the edge of things. We crossed the river by the road bridge which I had always thought of as the boundary of home, speeding between its high sides with the wind across us, and Francesca said,

—He'll be out of the hospital before too long, but he won't be able to manage alone. For a while, at least, and probably not ever.

I carried on looking out of the window, watching the ploughed fields flick by, the houses accumulate, the town begin.

—I went to the cottage this morning,

she said, and as she spoke she lifted a hand off the steering wheel, as though to pre-empt a protest that I didn't have the heart to make.

—He gave me the keys. He wanted some clothes and asked me to fetch them. The roof leaks.

—I know,

I said. Francesca went on,

—If it leaks enough to come through the ceiling then it must be a sizeable hole. And there's damp in other places, too. Rot maybe. If not, then there will be.

She waited to see if I would speak again, and when I didn't, said,

—Some of the window frames are rotten already. They need replacing.

I didn't want to say that there was almost certainly no money to fix these things, but the truth of it sat, squat, between us. Grandy had always maintained the cottage himself, but at some point, while I had been away, he must have stopped, or perhaps it had been slipping for years, always the last thing on the list.

We reached the hospital and Francesca drove into the car park, found a space, parked the car. She turned to face me.

—I need someone to live at the high house,

she said.

—I need someone to keep on top of the garden, and to look after things while I am away. To deal with deliveries. That sort of thing. I might be away a lot now. I can arrange an apartment for your grandfather on the ground floor. I'll have a bathroom put in for him. He could be quite self-contained. You could order the rest of the house as you wanted it, with the exception of a few of the bedrooms. We'll go over the details later, but you would be paid a retainer to act as caretaker, to keep the house in order and maintain the garden, particularly the vegetable garden.

—I'll need to speak to Grandy,

I said. Francesca smiled.

—If it makes you feel better, then tell your university you're deferring for a year. Call it a sabbatical. If there's any difficulty at all then I'll speak to them.

—I'll need to talk to Grandy,

I said again, and, keeping my back to her, got out of the car.

Francesca was right – Grandy could no longer manage by himself. His hip healed but he was left with stiffness, pain, a limp. He could walk with a stick, but not far. He was given a wheelchair by the hospital, and was discharged. There was no money for anything more than the most rudimentary home care, and no one else to take care of him but me. Without Francesca, we would have gone back to the cottage, and we would have lived on Grandy's tiny pension and whatever benefits I would have been able to claim for taking care of him, and things would have fallen apart around us, by degrees, until the storm came, and then we would have drowned, or perhaps Grandy would have drowned and I would have escaped to become one of the refugees – the people we see, sometimes, from the top field, trudging along what is left of the road. And I don't know what would have happened to me after that. Francesca knew that I didn't really have a choice, but she needed me, too, and Grandy. What would Caro have done, in the high house, by herself? How would she have dug the garden, lived, looked after Pauly? It is not enough to have an ark, if you do not also have the skills to sail it.

iii

The day Grandy was discharged, we went straight to the high house from the hospital. Francesca had done everything she had said she would. There was a suite of rooms waiting for

Grandy on the ground floor, a bedroom with a small bathroom attached, a walk-in shower, plenty of grab rails. The door to his room opened onto the kitchen, our main living space now, with a wood-fired range and French doors opening onto the paved terrace and the orchard, and it was this kitchen which Grandy really inhabited. He liked to sit and look out at the orchard, engrossed, as though he were watching the apples grow – and in the winter, sometimes, when dawn is near and I empty the grate, saving the still-warm embers to light the new day's fire, when I kneel on the hearth, my hands busy with the kindling, I forget that he is gone, and I think that I can feel him, behind me.

—Open the doors, Sal,

Grandy said when we came in, that first day, and I undid the catch and pushed them open to let in the air. He took a deep breath, and smiled – and I, too, could not suppress a lilt of joy, because even then, on a cold, grey day at the scrag end of the year, it was so beautiful.

Later, after we had unpacked his hospital bag and eaten sandwiches at the kitchen table, Grandy said,

—I won't go back to the cottage. It doesn't do to dwell.

I washed up the plates and the cups. I put them away in the cupboard, and asked him if there was anything else he wanted. I watched him make his way back into his room to rest, his slow limp aided by a stick – and I wish that I had offered him some kind of comfort, then, because it is true that the high house was beautiful, but that didn't make it home.

iv

I went back to the cottage by myself to pack our belongings into boxes, and a man came with a van from the town, just as Francesca had said he would, to drive them to the high house. A car would have done just as well. They would have fitted in the boot.

v

When Francesca came to visit, I showed her the new compost heap, the chicken coop, the potato beds that I had dug while Grandy watched, giving me directions from the fold-up chair which I had carried out for him. Afterwards, we walked down to the tide pool and stood side by side, Francesca and I, watching the mill wheel turn.

—I've been thinking that I should learn to drive,

I said, and expected that she would agree, because having no means of transport except my feet and the bike which I had found in one of the sheds meant that we were almost entirely cut off. Of course, we had all the vegetables and the fruit from the garden to eat, and the eggs from the chickens, and a van came once a month from the supermarket with supplies to be added to what was in the barn, but still I wished, at times, for another kind of freedom – the kind which is convenience, the ability to live one's life, in part, unplanned.

—No,

Francesca told me,

—I'd really rather you didn't,

and I was taken aback.

—It would make things easier,

I said,

—I'd be able to take Grandy to the hospital for his check-ups.

I didn't tell her that Grandy had refused to go the last three times that the hospital had sent patient transport for him and so, finally, they had written to say that he had been discharged from care against their advice. The tone of the letter had been terse, bordering on accusatory.

—Better learn to be without,

Francesca said.

vi

That night, sitting in bed in the dark with my laptop open on my knees, I looked at photographs of forests and the holes that had been torn in them, the gaping, sore-edged wounds where trees had been, the long, brown scars which were all that was left of the rivers. I tried to see these things as I thought Francesca did: not as a part of that long, slow slide, entropy, which grinds and grinds, which is beyond our intervention, is out of reach, winding us towards our end, but as something fresh and acute – a set of circumstances which could have been prevented, once, but now had gone beyond repair – but it was too much to bear. I closed my laptop, closed my eyes. Lay in the dark and waited for sleep to come, and when it did, I dreamed of nothing at all.

One day a boat arrived on the back of a lorry, a small wooden dinghy with oars and a single sail. Two men unloaded it into one of the empty sheds near the barn.

—What's it for?

I asked.

—We've already got a boat.

They shrugged.

—Search us, sweetheart. We're just doing what we were asked to.

Later, I told Grandy about it, saying,

—What use is it anyway, sat there in a shed? The sea's a mile away, and Francesca says no to a car, so it's not like we could get it to the harbour on a trailer.

It was only after the flood that I understood, and saw again how much thought Francesca had put into things, because Grandy's boat was wrecked with all the rest when the storm hit, forcing the water in over the land, destroying the shingle banks, the dyke, obliterating the harbour. Then we needed a boat, and Francesca, who had listened to Grandy's stories, had left us one, and made sure that it stayed safe, above the new waterline. And there wasn't far to drag it, then.

I stopped keeping track of the days. They had been reduced to their bare structure, a constant round of cooking and eating and washing up, and, in the spaces between these set points, the garden to be done, the chickens to be fed, the floors to be swept. I seemed to be busy all the time, but could never say, quite, what it was I had done that had taken up so many of the hours. At times I felt that I was drowning in the emptiness of it, and the boredom. One day, towards the end of winter, I went on a whim down to the church, because I wanted to see somewhere that wasn't the high house, the orchard or the vegetable garden, the tide pool, the beach. I hadn't realised that it was a Sunday, and so it was a shock to see a service in progress, the vicar in his vestments standing behind the altar rail, a handful of congregants on their knees. There was no choir today. I slipped into the back pew.

When the service was finished, after he had stood at the door while the others left, grasping their hands and wishing them well, the vicar came to sit next to me.

—It's been a long time,

he said.

—I've missed you. And your grandfather, of course. I hope he's well?

I shrugged.

—I forgot,

I said,

—that not everything had stopped. That it hasn't stopped for everyone, I mean, in the way that it's stopped for us. It was a shock to find you here, like seeing ghosts. Who were the people at the service?

—Passers-by. Pilgrims. They still come. People are afraid. Perhaps they think that God might hear them more clearly, if they are closer to the sea.

We sat in silence for a while, watching the light fade through the chancel window. At last, I said,

—All my life I have felt as though I were waiting for something to happen. For a change to come, one way or the other. And now everything has changed, and I am still waiting.

—Perhaps it is only your part in the world which has changed. Not yet the world itself.

—Will it?

—Well, I'm not sure it can go on as it is. But isn't that always the case? Change is the natural order of things.

I stood up.

—I must go,

I said.

—Grandy will be wondering where I am.

The vicar walked with me to the door, clasping my hand in the porch as he had the others', holding it inside both of his.

—Tell your grandfather he is not forgotten,

he said.

—Tell him I am here, still, if he should need me. And if not, I will come myself, one of these days.

ix

I walked back to the high house through the village. I hadn't been there for months, not since I had collected the last of Grandy's things from the cottage, and it was strange to see that it was there, when we were not. The walls still stood. The boats in the harbour bobbed at their moorings, and the gardens of the cottages, tended, presumably, by someone else, now that

Grandy no longer had the responsibility, still went on with their growing – but it was not the same as it had been. It felt, to me, as though it had been hollowed out, and now, instead of being a living place, it was a monument. Grandy had left, and so the last link to that past which he remembered, which had been governed by the weather, subject to tides, was severed. I couldn't argue that I would rather have had it otherwise. I couldn't say that I would have preferred their lives to mine – except that any loss, however it might be of benefit, is still a loss. And besides, there was the other thing – that all the safety and the comfort we had, the heating and the insulation, the gas hobs and electric lights, the things which happened when a switch was pressed, had their own cost. For decades, we had deferred payment, or passed the bill along, but soon it would be due, and who else was there left to pay?

x

Spring came, and we were alone. Francesca hadn't visited for months, and we had received no other word from her – only the deliveries, and the stipend which still came, monthly, into my bank account. The days lengthened and warmed. Grandy took control of the garden. Wrapped in blankets, sat in his chair in the kitchen, or on better days outside, he directed me. We overhauled the vegetable beds, the compost heap. He sent off for comfrey seeds to sow for fertiliser. We spent a long time watching the chickens, seeing which ones were the best layers.

—We'll need to grow corn for them,
he said.

—We can let them roam in good weather but they'll still need feeding in the winter. And we'll need another cockerel, if we're to keep the flock going.

He sent me down to the beach to collect mussel shells to grind for grit, which I scattered on the ground where the chickens liked to scratch.

—They need it to make eggshell,

he said,

—otherwise you get eggs with only a sack round them.

I didn't think until later that, as much as he was caring for the animals and for the garden, he might be teaching me.

xi

Francesca only came once more, arriving very late in the evening and without any warning. Her clothes were grubby and creased, as though she had been travelling for a long time, and she looked drawn.

—Your bed isn't made up,

I told her.

—I'll have to get sheets from the barn.

—Don't,

she said.

—I'll manage. I'm too tired, anyway.

She stayed one night, getting up early the next morning to walk round the house and garden, make a sort of inventory of the barn. Before she left, we stood together in the kitchen, side by side, looking out at the orchard.

—My stepdaughter might come,

she said,

—Caro. And my son. His name is Paul, but she calls him Pauly.

She hesitated, as though she wanted to ask me something – and I thought for a moment how hers was a life filled with departures, and I wondered if the returns made up for it, but decided that, on balance, they probably didn't. In the end she only said,

—Take care of them—

and then, after another pause,

—Please.

Pauly

A ND I remember walking, and walking, and walking, and the point at which I couldn't walk any more.

—I can't,

I said to Caro.

—I can't walk.

My feet hurt. My legs hurt. My throat was sore and I was tired, too tired to lift my legs.

—Sit down,

Caro said,

—sit down here, Pauly, and have a rest. I won't be long. Don't go anywhere.

I watched her scramble down the steep slope towards the wood, carrying our bags with her. I never doubted that she would come back, but even so I kept my eyes fixed on the place that she had disappeared, needing the time she was out of sight to be as short as possible.

i

Riding on Caro's back, I clung with my hands around her neck—

—Too tight, Pauly,

she said,

—too tight. You're choking me—

and although I tried to loosen them, because I didn't want to hurt her, it was hard, because I was afraid of falling. The train station was a very long time ago. I didn't know where we had been. I didn't know where we were going. It was getting dark. Perhaps I heard an owl.

ii

It is possible that, if things were otherwise, then the fact that I have no memory of my mother would seem a greater loss – but, as it is, her absence is only a smaller part of the whole. I have forgotten an entire world.

3

Sally

THE night Caro and Pauly arrived I lifted him down from her back and I carried him, so fast asleep that his head swung loose against my shoulder, through the dark orchard, into the house, and up to the bedroom which, months ago, Francesca had prepared for him. I put him down on the bed, and then I hesitated. I didn't know what to do next. I couldn't leave him as he was, his dirty clothes tangled round his body, the weight of his shoes making his feet splay oddly outwards – but nor could I bring myself to undress him, because, though a child, he was also a stranger, and the thought of stripping off his clothes without first asking his permission appalled me. He was too deeply asleep to rouse. It seemed extraordinary to me that a person should be able to sleep so soundly, but even when, getting him onto the bed, I had fumbled the drop so that he half-rolled, half-fell onto the mattress, one of his hands banging against the corner of the shelves which stood next to the bed, his eyelids had barely flickered. He only sighed, and shifted a little, and was still again. I stood and watched him. I wondered if I should call the girl, Caro, but she had seemed, when I had taken the boy from her, to be exhausted beyond the point of being sensible. Besides,

I had seen the news that afternoon, watching it on my laptop while Grandy slept in his chair in the kitchen. I knew that Francesca was dead.

In the end, I did the least that seemed necessary. I pulled off Pauly's shoes and socks, unzipped his coat. I nudged him onto his side. His chin was folded hard into his chest and I wondered, briefly, if he might somehow manage to suffocate, or if there was a risk of the toggles from his hood getting caught round his throat, but of course, I told myself, I was being absurd. I tucked the blanket around him, smoothed back the tangle of hair from his forehead, fetched a glass of water from the bathroom to leave beside the bed in case he woke and wanted it, and then, without knowing quite why, I leaned over the sleeping child and kissed the top of his head.

—Sleep well,

I whispered, and I tiptoed from the room.

i

—Did you take him to the toilet?

Grandy asked when I went downstairs and then, when I didn't answer, asked again, more sharply,

—Did you take him to the toilet, Sal?

—He was fast asleep—

Grandy sighed.

—You'll need to go back up, then.

—But he was fast asleep! I don't think I could wake him even if I wanted to.

—Then don't wake him. Pick him up and carry him to the bathroom. Sit him on the toilet. He'll go. He's a child, Sal. He needs you to look after him, not pet him, and he'll be desperate if he wets a strange bed.

I must have looked aghast, because Grandy relented a little.

—It's just a question of someone being in charge,
he said.

—It's a strange night all round, but all the more reason for those of us as can to do our best.

ii

After what Grandy had said, I began to worry that Pauly might wake in the night and, not knowing where he was, would cry out and not be heard. I tried to think of a solution, an open line between my laptop and my phone, perhaps, with one of them in Pauly's room, but in the end it seemed easier to make a bed for myself on the floor of the corridor outside his room, and so I did, pulling my duvet and my pillows down there, and some cushions from the sofa – only to find, when I woke, that at some point in the night he had crawled into it beside me. Now, he lay on his back, arms and legs spread out into a cross, face turned away from me, towards the wall. His right hand, fingers curling, rested against my shoulder. I lay and looked at it, and at the back of his head, the curve of his cheek, the rise and fall of his chest, and I thought it was miraculous, the trust that was written into every part of him. He seemed so fragile and so perfect, so small, so whole – but my neck ached from sleeping in the

space his body had left over and, as I tried to shift position,
I woke him up.

—Where's Caro?

he asked.

—Asleep,

I told him.

—She's very tired.

—Oh,

he said.

—What's for breakfast?

—I don't know. Shall we go and see?

and so we got up, shook ourselves, and made our way
downstairs, his hand, I found, resting neatly in my own.

iii

Grandy was already in the kitchen. He stood, leaning on his
stick, making coffee and toast.

—Good morning, Paul,

he said.

—I am Sal's grandfather. She calls me Grandy. Would you
like to do the same?

Pauly, standing by the table, nodded.

—Well then,

Grandy said,

—how about some breakfast?

We sat together, the three of us, eating our toast with
gooseberry jam.

—So, Paul,

Grandy asked, when the boy had finished and was sat licking butter from his hands,

—what do you like?

Pauly thought very hard, and then he said,

—Birds. I like birds the best.

Grandy laughed.

—In that case, young man, you will be easily pleased. Into the garden, now. Let's find some birds for you.

Standing up, Grandy waved his stick towards the double doors, and the two of them went out together, onto the terrace. I watched them while I cleared the breakfast things away, Grandy, his stick resting between his knees, sitting in the chair I had put out for him there when we had first come to the high house, and Pauly standing at his side. The boy was very quiet, until the wood pigeons and the blackbirds came down from the trees to scratch about in the grass of the orchard, and then he ran forward, chasing them, his arms stretched out as though he might, with luck or with a sudden burst of speed, be able to catch one of their firm bodies between his fingers – but they were always just out of reach, blustering away at the last moment, rising up into the air to land again, fussily, a few yards away, and so the game kept going, and I thought how ordinary it seemed. Already, Pauly was becoming ours.

iv

Sometimes, when summer light runs through the windows of the high house, when it lies in puddles on the floor, and when the air is still and there is quiet in all the rooms, then I find myself expecting, on stepping through a doorway, to see Pauly the way he was when he first came here. He had seemed, that first morning as he watched Grandy spreading toast with butter and jam, to have an air of patience that was very admirable to me. Standing in the kitchen, his hair tousled and his face rubbed with yesterday's dirt, his too-long trousers folded up unevenly at the ankles, he had waited for his breakfast as though he were waiting to see how things might work out, and would take whatever came to him with grace. It didn't occur to me, then, that this might be how all children are, because they must be used to not understanding things, to having the world happen around them while they wait to grow into it – and it didn't occur to me, either, that he might have been afraid, of Grandy or myself, or of this strange house in which he found himself, alone – but Pauly is still the only child that I have ever known, and I had nothing to compare him to then, and now I never will.

ν

—Caro,

I shouted through the door,

—this is Sally. Pauly is up. Do you have everything you need? There's breakfast downstairs if you want to eat. You must be hungry—

She didn't answer. I supposed that she must be still asleep, although it was getting on for mid-morning – but then,

I reasoned, she would be exhausted from the day before, and surely if she was awake then she would be worried about Pauly. I left her, and went back down the stairs.

vi

Pauly came with me to feed the chickens. They liked to scratch about in the grass around the cobnut tree, and that was where we scattered grain for them from the big bag that we stored, then, in the scullery, before we had to grow the grain ourselves and began to keep it in barrels in the barn.

—They need grit, too,

I said, and showed him the box of ground-up mussel shells,

—to help them put shells on their eggs—

and remembering how Grandy had said the same thing to me so recently I felt the colour rise to my cheeks.

—Are there any eggs?

he asked, and I took him to the coop to see. I showed him how to lift up the wooden flaps on the backs of the houses, how to chivvy away the broody birds and steal their eggs out from under them.

—We'll have them for lunch,

I said.

—Caro, too?

—Caro needs to rest.

We left the coops and walked back towards the house. In each of his hands, Pauly carried an egg.

—When I was a boy,

Grandy said,

—on summer evenings you could hear the bitterns call. They boomed, you know. Like this—

he let out a sort of deep hooting noise which scared the crows up out of the hedge. Pauly laughed. They were out on the terrace again, waiting for the lunch to finish cooking. I went upstairs to knock a second time on the door of Caro's bedroom, but, even when I called out, loudly, to say that there was food waiting, she didn't reply. The day drew on. After lunch I read to Pauly from one of the books on the shelf in his bedroom, and then I took him to the tide pool, where he splashed about in the shallow water at its edge.

—Does it really make electricity?

he asked, pointing at the waterwheel.

—It does,

I said, and tried to explain the mechanics of it until, bored by my discursive tone, Pauly interrupted me.

—Look, Sal! That seagull is eating a crab! It has the legs hanging out of its beak!

In the evening I made him have a bath, and dressed him in the pyjamas I had found in the drawers of the cupboard in his bedroom, freshly washed, unworn, one size too big, as though they had been bought to allow for growth.

—Is Caro still asleep?

he asked.

—I think so,

I said,

—but maybe we could go and say goodnight to her anyway?

He nodded, and we went to stand outside her door.

—Goodnight, Caro,

Pauly called, and, satisfied I thought, went back to bed.

viii

—Caro,

I shouted, banging hard on the wooden boards of her door.

—Caro. For Christ's sake. You haven't eaten anything all day. Pauly's asking for you. Caro. Are you ill in there? Unlock the door. Will you please unlock the door—

And all day, in the background, the thought of what Pauly didn't seem to know: Francesca and his father, their hotel torn open by the sea, their bodies and belongings churning in the water.

ix

I left a tray of breakfast outside Caro's room and, later, came back to find that the food had been eaten and the dirty plate and cutlery put back on the tray in the corridor.

—This isn't a bloody hotel—

I shouted. Then, more quietly,

—I don't know anything about children.

x

I took Pauly to the beach.

—Take three changes of clothes,

Grandy said,

—and a jumper, because he'll get cold after he's been in the sea.

I felt ridiculous, walking across the dunes in the hot sun with my stuffed rucksack on my back. Pauly raced ahead, excited.

—Sal! Sal! I can see the sea.

We found a place to sit, laid out the blanket I had brought. Pauly stripped off his shoes and socks, his trousers and his pants, and ran in just a T-shirt towards the sea, and it was only then that I thought to ask, calling my question to his retreating back,

—Pauly, can you swim?

Still running, he shook his head, and I scrambled after him, grabbing at his hand as he reached the waves, which were stiff despite the sunshine. For half an hour he leapt about, his T-shirt quickly soaked and taken off to leave him naked, running in and out, jumping the foaming edges, his body milk-pale and bony, and I was gripped with absolute terror in case he should trip and fall and somehow contrive to be swept away.

Afterwards, we ate the sandwiches Grandy had made for us, Pauly shivering in the jumper I had brought which wasn't thick enough, a towel wrapped round his legs, the skin under his fingernails blueish from the cold. When the tide had slid out far enough, we went rockpooling, scrambling over the stone outcrops looking for crabs, finding a shoal of tiny fish hiding among the bladderwrack, a sea anemone, some whelks. Then I became terrified again, this time imagining how Pauly might slip and tear open his bare legs on the sharp parts of shell or shingle, the dread that I should fail to keep him safe all the time competing with the joy it was to watch his joy – and when, that evening, I put him in the bath and saw the reddening skin across his shoulders where the sun had caught it, I couldn't bring myself to tell Grandy that I had forgotten the sun cream.

xi

How quickly the status quo establishes. We fall into a pattern, and life is set. That evening, opening my laptop after Pauly and Grandy were in bed, I found that the news was still full of the American storm, the devastation and the search for survivors. Francesca's photograph appeared between drone footage of torn buildings and flooded streets which showed the water lying still and calm and deep across the places people had thought they owned. The commentary was flat with shock. This was something new, it seemed, this incursion of water into homes. It was the beginning of some second phase, a turning point – except, of course, that it was really only more of the same. We had been watching people drown for years, and the only difference was that they had always been a long way off from us, before. We sent money, perhaps, if the pictures were bad enough, and then we went on as we always had. Their deaths, although we didn't like to say so, were not really a disaster to us, because disaster would only come when it had our own face on it – and now, here it was. Drowned shopping malls and smashed double glazing. Recently upgraded family saloon cars turning circles in currents running down residential streets. Splintered garden fences floating through the forecourts of office blocks. The people who now sat in shelters, whose faces were stiff with shock, wore our own clothes. They sat in rows in upstate schools and churches, corridors with brightly coloured posters, and they had brought their dogs with them, and duvets with cartoon characters on the covers to wrap their frightened children in. Surely, they should have been exempt. Surely Francesca should have been – but already I could feel that we were getting used to it. On my laptop screen, a man explained that much should have been done earlier to protect such a low-lying city. Its inhabitants had baulked at the cost, or they had not wanted their view of the sea impeded by defences. It was, in some way we were still grasping at, their own fault. *There are lessons to be learned*, he said.

I shut my laptop and reached for the glass of water on my bedside table. I thought of Pauly, and wondered if, the next day, I should take him to the village for an ice cream.

xii

Pauly, standing in the kitchen in his pyjamas, said,
    —Where's Caro? I want Caro.

His hands were balled into fists, the muscles in his legs and arms so tightly clenched that he was shaking.

—Pauly?

I asked,

—what's brought this on?

Grandy frowned at me and shook his head, said,

—Let's go and find her, shall we?

He limped out of the kitchen towards the stairs, beckoning me to follow. I picked Pauly up, swinging him onto my hip and thinking, as I did so, how quickly I had become accustomed to his weight. He clung to me, his arms around my neck, his legs wound tightly round my waist, and as I went to follow Grandy up the stairs I heard him whisper,

—I thought she must have gone away,

and felt such extraordinary shame because, all through the days since he had come, I had believed that he was happy. I had thought he was too busy to think of Caro, or that he was too young to feel her absence – and all the time, it seemed, he had been thinking that he had been left behind.

Grandy hammered hard on Caro's door.

—Enough,

he shouted to her,

—that is enough.

xiii

It is at this time of year, in the early weeks of spring, that Caro is at her worst. These are hard months, it is true. The days are still short, and there is cold in the air, frost in the mornings, and we must eke out the last of our stored food while we wait for the first new crops to come through, and often we are hungry – a constant, grinding state of want that is exhausting, like being always cold, which we also are. Still, though, for Pauly and me it is the turning point. We can see the end of the bad weather coming, the way the notches on the branches swell to buds. We feel lighter, as the winter's trudge turns to a final sprint – but Caro seems to shrink. She loses hope. Each year, the winter wears away at her. She is stretched out by the dark and cold. The skin on her hands cracks and bleeds, and she has chilblains which must be looked after carefully if they aren't to become infected. We have to watch her, reminding her not to put her feet too close to the fire, not to rest her hands on the stove or to wrap them round the scalding mugs of herb tea that she makes. In the evenings, when we have done as much work as the dark and the weather will allow, I put out bowls of warm salt water for her to soak her hands and feet in, and then afterwards I watch her pat them dry, making sure she doesn't rub, and I help her to get clean socks on without doing more damage to her skin. These things, this physical sort of care, I can manage, but I can't be patient with her. I can't sit quietly next to her like Pauly does, holding her hand, stroking her hair. He whispers to her, and I am jealous, in part because I don't know what he is saying, but also because I see in him something that I lack – the capacity for gentleness, for empathy or understanding. Then I remember those days when Caro wasn't there and how, at the time, it seemed to me as though, when I let Pauly get into bed with me, when I explained away Caro's absence and sent him out to play in the garden, I did nothing but try to fill the gaps she had left behind – but we are grown up, now, and I think that what I was really trying to do, in those few days after Caro and Pauly arrived, was to take him away from her.

Caro

I ARRIVED at the high house and found Sally waiting and it was as if, after all the horrible efforts of the day, after the train journey and the small humiliations of the town, after standing in the pub watching the news and walking so far with Pauly, I had at last been let off the hook. She took Pauly from me, carried him away, and I was not responsible any more. I followed her into the high house and sat down on a chair in the hallway, too exhausted to do more than wait to be told what I should do next. After a while, Grandy came, leaning on a stick.

—Caro,

he said,

—I am Sal's grandfather.

I didn't ask what these two strangers were doing in the high house, when I had thought it would be empty. I didn't ask why the house should be so warm and well looked-after, or why they should seem to have been expecting us. I found that I had no energy for surprise. Grandy said,

—I would show you to your room, but I find the stairs too difficult, so could you find your own way, if I tell you where to go? I think that lots will have changed since you were here last.

He gave me directions and I followed them, found the bathroom, where I washed my hands and face, and then the bedroom, its window open to let the night in, the smell of air and earth and, on the edge of it, the sea. A white cotton nightshirt was folded on a chair and I stripped off my clothes and put it on. I got into bed. Sal brought me a plate of cheese on toast and I ate it. I didn't ask about Pauly. Somewhere, I thought, he was safe, and that was enough to know, because I was so tired, and to ask where, to find out, would have forced me from the bed to go to him.

i

I have come to understand, lately, how need is complicated. It is a knotted loop which, although unpicked, does not unwind. I think about it, when night comes, and I feel my mind starting to crawl across my skin – how, when we say that someone needs us, often what we mean is that we need them, or need their need for us. It gives us our position. It shows us where our edges are. The next morning, when I woke, my hands and face were swollen from the previous day's sun, and from a night of heavy sleep. The muscles in my calves and thighs ached, and across my arms and back, too, where I had carried Pauly. I crept to the bathroom, one hand against the wall to steady myself because my legs felt weak and unreliable. The house was quiet. I had a shower, my arms too sore to lift but the water rinsing off the dirt anyway, and after that I put the nightshirt back on, went back along the corridor, returned to bed. My desire to see Pauly, to pick him up and feel the weight of him, the warmth, was a physical thing, a want like hunger is, or cold – but what I wanted more was to be left alone. I knew that, when I saw him, I would have to tell him about Francesca, and about father, and I would not be able to be alone again afterwards. I would have to be present for him, to soak up his sadness and whatever else came with it, his anger or confusion, and I would have to watch for the moments when those things broke through, and be patient with him. I would have to bite my tongue to keep my temper when he lost his, and tell him afterwards that this was how it was for everyone, the pain of losing coming out in sudden bursts of rage, but it would be a lie, because that is not how it could be for me. I would have to hold my anger in, to make myself safe for him, and I was very tired, and wanted to think of no one except myself. Francesca had gone, and she had left me with Pauly as she had always left me with Pauly, trading on my love for him – and, after all, he would find me when he wanted me. Surely any moment he would come through the door. Surely any moment I would hear his feet in the corridor, his voice calling my name, and the stillness would be broken, and I would be taking care of him again.

ii

I heard his voice, but it wasn't in the corridor, or on the stairs. It came instead drifting up from the garden, in through the open bedroom window, and he sounded happy. I heard him laugh.

Sally banged on the door to say that breakfast was ready. I didn't answer, and she went away.

iii

I stood at the window and looked down. Below me was the brick terrace outside the kitchen, and then the orchard, the grass between the trees kept long, Grandy would tell me later, so that clover would colonise it, and feverfew and meadow clary, yarrow, self-heal, and all the other flowers which would bring what was left of the pollinators, remnants of that buzzing cloud, to swarm down through shafts of sunlight, searching for the flowers' well-marshalled sweetness. Past the orchard there was the hedge, and then the vegetable garden. I could see the red-flowered runner beans on their high canes, the artichoke bush we lost to frost three winters later. I could see the hen coop and the well. I could see the path which led down to the tide pool, and Sally on it, walking back towards the house with Pauly, his legs bare, his hair wet, his hand in hers.

iv

Afterwards, Sal told me that she had brought Pauly up to say goodnight to me, and that though he had called out to me through the door I had not answered. She said that he had wanted me, then, and that I had ignored him – but I know that if I had heard him I would have got out of bed. I would have opened the door to let him in so that he might clamber up to lie next to me as he always had, so close, while the evening folded itself down into the night. I didn't hear him. Perhaps I was asleep.

Hours passed and I was furious. Anger was a hard nut in my throat and I could neither cough it up nor swallow it down. I lay, as dawn broke on the second day, in a bed which had become tangled and musty, and I counted the injustices – father gone, and Francesca – Pauly and I left behind – the high house inhabited by strangers. I had been a child here but now it had been remade, so that although the whole house, when in the night I had got out of bed and crept around it, had hummed with familiarity, it was the familiarity of a missed step. Each corner was a lurch. Each window a practised deception. Known doors opened onto strange rooms. Corridors betrayed. This was not the house I had come to as a child, where I had run from room to room, where I had played hide-and-seek by myself, or waited for father, nagging him to take me to the tide pool, the beach, the ice-cream van, and its new shape was part of a plan that no one had thought to share with me. How much time must Francesca have spent planning it, this haven – whole days when, left behind, I took Pauly to the playground, cooked his meals and washed his clothes, packed his nursery bag, read stories to him, knotted my life to his. I imagined how she must have walked around the house and the garden, thinking what would be required – and when she had wanted someone to live there, to be its caretaker, she had chosen Sally. Father knew. They must have meant to come here together, and I wondered when she had changed her plans. Was it only as the water rose around her, as the wind began to make the building creak, that she had been forced to reconsider, so that instead of her here with Pauly, it was me? – And, still, if it hadn't been for the journey I might as well have stayed behind, because Pauly had Sally to look after him now.

vi

Sal brought me food on a tray, and I ignored her, and then after she was gone I ate the food and left the tray outside, hoping that it would hurt.

vii

Perhaps, I thought, Francesca hadn't even meant for Pauly to come. Perhaps it was only her and father that the high house had been made for. And perhaps it wasn't she who had changed the plans – perhaps it was father alone who, at the last moment, had thought of us, while Francesca had called him away from the phone—

The thought of father was unbearable. I could feel the shape of the empty space his hands had left behind. I could hear the silence where his voice should be. I wanted him, and he was gone.

viii

These were the things which I thought about all day long as I lay in bed, sunlight coming and going, Pauly coming and going, the sound of his voice rising quietly or more loudly from the house or from the garden. I grasped my wrongs around me like a comforter and let them warm me until, at last, Grandy came.

—That is enough,

he said from the corridor, his voice hard and loud. I got out of bed and went to the door, and when I opened it the sight of Pauly in Sally's arms, his face crumpled from the effort of not crying, came on me like a whipping.

—Oh god, Pauly,

I said,

—I'm sorry.

He leaned towards me, reaching up his arms, and I took him, went back into my room, closed the door behind us with a kick of my foot. He started to cry, and then I was crying. We stood in the middle of the floor, tears running down our cheeks.

—It's all right, Pauly,

I said,

—I'm here—

I sat down and pulled him into my lap, folding his legs and arms so that he still fitted there, tightly, as he had done when he was a baby.

—I'm here,

I said,

—I'm here. I love you, it's all right—

and he nodded, but he didn't stop crying, and I knew that it was not all right. I had made him come to me, my tiny brother, who was a child. His need for me was clear and simple. He had only wanted me to be present, to watch him and, by watching him, to make him safe, and I had not done it. I had brought him to this place that he had not wanted to come to, where everything was strange, and I had left him with strangers, and I had thought that I was the one who had been wronged.

Sally

C ARO opened the door and Pauly reached out to her at once.
—Oh god, Pauly,

she said,

—I'm sorry,

and I wanted to turn and carry Pauly straight back down the stairs again, but Pauly was leaning so far towards her that I thought I'd drop him, so I put him down, and he ran to her. She closed the door. I went to bang on it again but Grandy shook his head.

—Leave them be,

he said.

—But,

I hissed, hoping that she would hear me through the door,

—she can't just say she's sorry and then think that makes it okay. She can't just dump a child on us whenever she wants to. How long are they staying? I'm not bringing her any more meals up here.

Grandy turned and started walking slowly back towards the stairs, his hand on the wall to steady himself.

—Be kind, Sal,

he said, and I felt his rebuke like a slap across my cheek.

Caro

W E lay side by side on the bed, staring at the ceiling, Pauly's head resting on my arm, my hand curled around his waist. I tried to think of a way to soften what I had to say, some trick to make the words less absolute, but I knew that to do so would be to lie. I wondered if I should tell him that there was still a chance that father and Francesca were not dead. After all, no bodies had been found. They had not been pulled from the water and counted – but that small gap was not hope. The space between what we knew and what was certain was a coward's truth. I said,

—Pauly, I have to tell you something that is very difficult. It's something very sad. The building that father and your mother were staying in was destroyed in a storm the night before we came here. They were in it when it happened, and I don't think there is any way they could have survived.

Pauly was silent, but I knew he had heard me, because I felt the way the muscles tensed around his bones. At last he said,

—There's a beach, Caro. I went there yesterday. I saw a hermit crab,

and so we got up, Pauly and I, and I let him show me the house, and the garden, the tide pool, the beach, all these places which in my absence he had taken possession of so that still, now, years later, they often feel more his than they are mine. I bought us ice creams from the ice-cream van which still stood, that last summer, in the car park by the harbour wall, and we ate them by the river, watching the boats bob gently at their moorings. The tide was half out.

—Look, Caro,

Pauly said, pointing at a flock of black-and-white birds who were picking their way through the mud,

—oystercatchers—

Afterwards, we ran together down to the sea and waded out into it, into water which was cold and very clear, and I felt joy come, in from the waves and from the feel of Pauly's hand in mine, from the way he knew the names of all the birds, his own peculiar personhood, and I could have stayed that way forever, on the beach in the afternoon, but time always passes. The sun goes in. We must pack up our things and go home.

Sally

I SAW Pauly leading Caro out through the garden.
—They seem happy now, anyway,
I said.
—Sal,
Grandy said,
—they've just lost their parents.
—They've got each other,
I said. Grandy gave me a long look.
—And you've got me.

i

At teatime, Caro helped to set the table, letting Pauly show her
the drawer where the cutlery was kept, the cupboard with the
glasses in. Afterwards, she stood next to me and dried while
I did the washing-up.
—Where does the colander live?
she asked, and I showed her.
—Did you often come here, before?
I asked.
—Not for years,

she answered.

—Not since I was small. It's different now. I didn't know—and then,

—Thank you for looking after us. I didn't know that there was anyone here. It was a shock. I thought Pauly and I would be on our own. I didn't know what Francesca had been doing. Or my father—

I felt generous, then. I wanted to be able to offer her something, to say to her that perhaps they were still alive. I wanted to be able to give comfort, even if it were false, but she had seen the pictures just as I had. Besides, generosity can be another kind of power – like charity, like not grieving, like knowing where the crockery is kept. I said nothing, but passed her another plate to dry.

Pauly

CARO came with me to the beach and I showed her all the things I had discovered – the rock pools, the game of running into the waves and out again, the place where there was a pile of boulders that could be climbed – and when we got back to the high house, while Caro was helping Sally with the dinner, Grandy let me go into his bedroom and look through the cupboard he kept his precious things in. I found a wooden box which was full of odds and ends – buttons and old postcards, cogs from ancient watches, a pair of kid-leather gloves folded up in tissue paper – and I emptied it out onto the floor and sat, sorting through it, until the others called me back into the kitchen to eat. Sally had made a rhubarb crumble and put so much sugar in it that Grandy said,

—My teeth ache just looking at it.

—What teeth?

Sally asked. He laughed, and as he did so I tried to see inside his mouth, in case Sally was right and he really didn't have any teeth. We sat down at the table. Grandy did not say, as he had on the other evenings since I had come to the high house, *Now then, Paul. Tell me what mischief you've made today—*

but instead he spoke to Sally, saying,

—If the weather goes on like this, we'll have to think of some way to water the orchard.

I felt them watching me, even while they weren't looking at me. I felt their worry, and I wished I could explain to them that there was no need for it. It was a relief, what Caro had told me about my parents, like running full tilt into the cold sea is a relief, because afterwards you no longer have to wait for it to happen. My parents had always been absent, and though I don't remember them, I remember how it felt to wait for them – how each night I would go to sleep wondering if in the morning they would be there, or gone. I remember how exhausting it was, being constantly pleased to see some-body – and now, at last, I knew where I stood. They were gone completely, and nothing was really any different, except that I could stop waiting for them to come back.

i

Something was wrong with Caro, but I didn't know what it was. Sometimes, while I was playing in the garden, she came out of the house and, kneeling on the ground, she opened her arms for me to run into them, and then she swung me into the air, over and over, until I thought that I would cry if she didn't call a halt to the game, because that was what she was supposed to do, tell me that it was enough – and at other times I stood beside her in the kitchen calling her name, but she didn't even turn her head to look at me.

—Caro,

I said, as we sat at the table in the morning, eating our breakfast,

—can we go to the beach today? Will you take me to the village? Can we walk out over the marsh? I want to count the swans.

I was sure that if I could keep her busy, if I could hold her attention for long enough, then it would stop feeling as though half of her was elsewhere.

—Not this morning, Pauly,

she said.

—Maybe Sally will take you,

and after she had finished her toast she went into the hallway and put on the pair of running shoes which she had found, left behind by Francesca, in the cupboard under the stairs. I followed her, watching her do up the laces, check the tightness of them, stretch. I watched her go out through the front door and then, from the window, I watched her break into a jog on the path towards the tide pool, speeding up as she disappeared through the hedge. Grandy had come out from the kitchen and was standing behind me.

—You're a kind boy,

he said,

—but it's not your job to make your sister happy.

iii

I was in the bath, and Caro was washing my hair, pouring water over my head with a mug to get the suds out.

—Heavens, Pauly,

she said,

—your ears are full of sand.

I gave my head a shake to get her to stop poking me.

—Caro,

I asked,

—do you miss father?

—Of course I miss him,

she answered, but I felt her fingers clench where she was holding my shoulders. I asked,

—Do you miss Francesca?

—Time to get out of the bath, now,

she said,

—it's late,

and she reached down to the end, and pulled out the plug.

Sally

ONE morning I came into the kitchen and found a man there, waiting. He was wearing a suit, a clean white shirt, clean leather shoes. He looked polite. He looked relaxed. He looked like someone who ought to be in charge, and I was suddenly aware how tangled my hair was from too much salt and not enough brushing, and how my hands and face, my feet, were dirty from the garden.

—Hello,

he said,

—the gate was open. And the door, so I came in. A liberty, I'm afraid, but I was passing by – I'm looking for Caroline.

Caro

S AL said,
   —There's a lawyer here to see you.
   —I don't want to see anyone,
   I told her, and turned away.
   —He's here about Francesca. You should see him, Caro,
   but I wouldn't. Francesca was gone. She had made the high
house in secret. She had built herself a sanctuary and then, at
the last moment, she had sent me there instead. She had cast
us off, Pauly and me. She had gone, and she had taken father
with her, and I wanted no part of anything that she might
have left to say to me.

Sally

I STOOD on the landing and counted to ten before I went back downstairs because the urge to slap Caro was almost overwhelming and I didn't want the lawyer in his fancy suit to see that I was angry.

—She doesn't want to speak to you,

I said.

—Ah.

We stood and looked at one another and, in my head, I cursed Caro, in whom unhappiness so often seemed to look like selfishness, the inability to understand that things she felt herself unable to do would have to be done by someone else. It was hard, at times, to remember the other part of her – the way she had been when she first arrived, stumbling up the path from the tide pool, Pauly asleep on her back, doing, when left no other choice, what needed to be done.

—Is it important?

I asked. The lawyer made non-committal noises that suggested that, of course, it might be, but he couldn't say one way or the other to me.

—Could you talk to me?

I asked,

—or to my grandfather?

because I thought he might prefer to speak to someone older. I tried not to think of the grubby vest and shorts I wore, my bare feet, the dirt on my hands and on my knees where I had been weeding, the scratches on my arms from picking the early gooseberries with Pauly to make jam. The lawyer looked around the kitchen before he answered, and then he looked back at me and smiled.

—There's no need, really. I'm only here because I have sent letters which have not been answered, and I was concerned – and also, I have to admit, curious. I was in the area, you know. I noticed a letterbox on the wall by the gate as I came in. It seemed full. Perhaps you might look there, and if you have any questions you can be in touch. Your sister will need to sign the forms.

—She's not my sister,

I said.

—No.

He smiled again, and his smile was kinder than his suit.

—Well—

He turned and went back the way he must have come, out through the kitchen doors, waving as he did so.

i

—It seems that Francesca set up a trust,

Grandy said, the papers spread out before him on the table. I sat beside him, fishing out the bits that needed signing. Caro was out again, running. I had tried to tell her about the papers, but she was already lacing up her trainers.

—You look at them,

she said.

—I think we really need you to be there, too, Caro.

—You look,

she said again, loudly, silencing my voice with her own. And then she was gone.

ii

I turned over paper after paper and the truth, which since the night when Caro and Pauly had arrived at the high house had hovered, almost present – since before, even, when Grandy had fallen and Francesca had come to fetch me – was now made obvious. This was what Francesca had intended all along. She had built the high house for Pauly, not for herself. It was a sanctuary, and Grandy and I were in the fabric of it, like the generator or the well, the barn, the boxes of seeds and the compost bins – a way of ensuring the safety of her son.

—Caro will be back soon,

I said to Grandy. Pauly was sitting on the floor in the corner, building houses out of some wooden blocks that Grandy had made for him, and I heard him stand up.

—Go and wait for her,

Grandy said,

—and take her to the barn. Show her. She needs to see for herself. Paul and I will get the tea on, won't we, Paul?

Pauly said,

—I want to go and meet Caro.

—Not this time,

Grandy told him, kindly, and, taking his hand, said,

—You'll see her soon enough, young man. Let Sally see her first. And anyway, I need your help to fetch some eggs.

iii

I stood by the hedge and waited for Caro, watching the shadows stretch. The summer was still young, then. It still had the freshness spring had left it. Things grew, and were green. There was no sign, yet, of the exhaustion which would come later, when everything was dusty and worn, and we waited and waited for the first frost to come and put an end to it. Bees hung over the few open flowers of the honeysuckle. A butterfly flickered from the grass. I saw Caro run towards me, round the tide pool. I saw her notice me. I saw her choose not to turn or hesitate. Her feet were steady, calmly paced. She came to a halt in front of me, and said,

—What do you want?

—Nothing,

I told her.

—To take you to the barn, that's all.

She shrugged, but when I walked away, she followed me. We went around the house, past the vegetable garden, past the chicken coop where Pauly, bent low to the ground, was searching for eggs.

—They've started laying on the ground,

I said,

—which seems absurd when they have such nice huts.

Caro shrugged again. We went into the barn. Inside, I led her between the stacks, past all the shelves and boxes of supplies which Francesca had left, labelled, protected, to keep us safe, right to the back, where the clothes were kept. We stopped.

—Well?

she said, but I knew that she had seen it. We stood and looked at the boxes of shoes, plimsolls for the summer and stout boots for winter, two pairs in a box with Grandy's name on, ten pairs apiece for me and Caro, and, for Pauly, a whole shelving stack, boxes and boxes in a variety of sizes.

—Of course,

Caro said,

—we don't know what size his feet will be.

There were no boots for Francesca. There were none for Caro's father, either.

—I wonder if he knew,

she said.

—I suppose he must have done. I wonder if they talked about it.

She turned and began to walk away, back out of the barn and towards the house.

—I'll see if Grandy needs any help with dinner,

she said, and I let her go.

Caro

Later, after Sally had shown me the barn, I went back by myself, because I needed to be sure. I walked between the shelves and shelves of crates, past the food supplies and the spare tools, the clothes and shoes, to the very back, where there was a corner of things for Pauly, and then I knelt down, feeling the cold concrete beneath my knees. I stayed for a long time, staring at them – the boxes of felt-tip pens, the reams of paper, chalks, playing cards, boxes of Lego – and in the silent barn I felt love come off the shelves like heat. I felt Francesca, planning, all through the autumn and the winter, while I thought she had abandoned us. She must have known, quite clearly, how unnecessary these items were. She must have known that the space could be better used to store another hundred light bulbs, or sailcloth for the boat, but I think she couldn't bear it, quite – to build a future for her son in which there was nothing for him but that which would keep him alive. Perhaps she wondered, sometimes, if it wouldn't be better to let him go with the rest – and when that happened, I wonder if she found herself adding another thing to this corner, a kit for making a dinosaur out of plywood, a rubber ball, a sheaf of stickers in the shape of stars. Still, though, the thought remains: if there had not been Pauly – if there had only been me, and Pauly had not been born – would Francesca still have made the high house? And, if I had not loved Pauly the best – if it had been her that he had spoken to instead of to me, if it was her bed that he had clambered into when he woke up in the night, or her that he had pointed out the birds to, hers the hand that his had grasped – would Francesca, then, have stayed behind for him?

4

Pauly

S UMMER unspooled. Days went on forever, morning being so far from night. I remember how the hours were full of details, the way the fine hairs stood out blonde against the brown skin of my legs, the way the sea felt as I ran into it – its pure cold, the slap of waves against my skin. I remember Grandy showing me the compost heap, pointing out the creatures that lived in it, the slugs and the earwigs, the tangles of pink worms. The wonder of it – I could have stood for hours, lifting up the mess of rotting rhubarb leaves, of grass clippings and sticks, to see what I had disturbed, the tiny bodies scurrying or shrinking or creeping away from the light. I remember the birds, and how it seemed to me that we hovered on the edge of understanding, and that they were only waiting for me to be still enough before they would come close to me, and speak.

Caro

I WAITED for Pauly to ask me about the high house, about what we were doing there. I waited for him to ask me when we would be going home, but although his questions were endless, they were not about the things which we had left behind. Instead, they were about the names of birds or of flowers, or whether the leafy, cabbage-looking plants which grew between the dunes were edible, or how lobsters were caught.

—I don't know,

I said to him, ten times a day.

—But Caro—

—Ask Grandy. He'll know—

and off he went, enthusiasm in his ankles and his elbows, running up the path to where Grandy sat at the edge of one of the vegetable beds, pointing with his stick to show Sally the correct spacing for the planting-out of cabbages.

i

—I love you, Pauly,

I said as I tucked him in at night, first the left-hand side of the bed and then the right.

184

—Tighter, Caro!

he ordered and I said,

—You know that you can talk to me if you want to—

but he only shuffled his way down the bed until the cover came up almost to his nose.

—You'll come and check on me, won't you?

he asked. I nodded.

—Promise?

—Of course—

because somewhere in the chaos of the journey from the city to the high house, and the days I had been absent, we had lost the habit of sharing a bed.

ii

I sat on a towel and watched Sally teaching Pauly to swim.

—Kick!

I heard her shout,

—you have to kick your legs—

A sudden churn of spray flew up around Pauly. Sally had her arms around his waist, out where the water was thigh-deep, the bottom sandy, and he was trying hard but couldn't manage more than a frantic, full-body wriggling. Later, when Pauly got cold, he would come and sit next to me, and I would wrap him in a towel and feel him close and pass him sandwiches. Midsummer had come, and there was a balance to things. I saw that Sally was a counterweight, the other half of me that Pauly needed.

Pauly

S ALLY says,
—Do you remember how you kept running off, onto the heath or down to the beach, and then Caro and I would have to come and look for you? We'd be terrified, every time, that you'd turn up face down in the tide pool, or in a ditch on the marsh, until we found you hiding in a tree, or turning over logs on the dunes to look for sandhoppers, and you'd just look up at us and say something like, *But I wanted to know what the sea looked like.*

Caro says,
—I think of that summer as so happy. Why would that be?
—The weather was so good,
Sally answers,
—and we were so pleased with ourselves. I made jam – do you remember? I boiled it too long and it set like rubber, but still I thought I was very bloody clever for doing it, and now we'd always have jam because we had fruit, but obviously we'd had to buy the sugar. And Grandy was there, telling us what to do.

Then we are all quiet, because we are thinking of Grandy.

Caro

THE sun shone on us and we waited. Sally and Grandy weeded the garden. Pauly fed the chickens. I ran. What else was there to do? As the weeks went on, I stopped watching Pauly so closely. I stopped thinking of him as hurt—

This truth has been laid bare for us, now. We see it every time we fall – every time a knife slips, or a splinter finds its way beneath the skin – that we will either get better, or we won't. We need only let the time pass to see if, this time, we will heal.

Sally

THERE are still good days. They come like shafts of light through heavy cloud, touching the ground with gold.

—Let's have bread,

Caro says – and so, because these good days are worth celebrating, we take out a small measure of the wheat flour which Pauly grinds and stores each year, a luxury because making it takes up time and affords us comparatively little return, and we make the best bread we can with one of the small packets of yeast, long past their best, which are in the barn, and we eat it spread with jam, another luxury because we have so little sugar and must instead preserve by pickling or by salting. Pauly makes the bread.

—Oh, Pauly,

Caro says,

—another triumph,

and we fall about laughing because the bread is horrible – its texture is heavy, and it turns to a sort of paste when chewed.

—I remember bag bread,

she says.

—It was so soft! And so white. I used to toast it for your breakfast, Pauly, and spread it so thick with butter that it ran down your wrists. You touched the wall, once, in the city house, and left a perfect greasy handprint on the wallpaper. I had to move a chest of drawers in front of it to stop Francesca noticing.

    —I'm sorry my offering is substandard,

Pauly says, with mock affront.

    —It tastes fine to me.

Pauly

SOMETIMES I think that Caro and Sal forget all the things I don't know. There was a time, when I was seven or eight years old, when I became preoccupied with money. I would spend whole afternoons searching in the river mud for coins, for purses and credit cards, all the things which the storm and its long aftermath had pulled into the water, and I brought them home as treasure. Caro didn't like to look at them, but Sal laughed and found me a box to keep them in, a wooden one with brass hinges and a small key.

—Where did it come from?

I asked.

—It was Grandy's,

she said.

—He kept his special things in it.

I liked to sit and make piles with the coins, taking them in and out of the purses. At lunchtime, I carried a fistful to the kitchen, put them on the table.

—What's that?

asked Caro, frowning.

—It's to pay for my lunch.

Afterwards, Sal gave them back to me.

—But I gave them to Caro,

I said.

—Caro doesn't want them. Anyway, how will you pay for your dinner if you've given all of your money to Caro?

—I'll get some more from the river,

I told her, and ran off, back out into the garden, down to the river to look.

i

The post office was another puzzle. Its unknowns ran into one another. I couldn't imagine living far enough away from some-one that you would need to post a letter to them. I couldn't imagine what you would want to say. Sal said,

—Supposing you wanted new trousers. You could order them, and then they would arrive in the post.

—But if I want new trousers,

I said,

—I can go to the barn and find a pair that fit.

—Well, yes. But imagine that you wanted a different colour maybe—

All of my clothes are green or blue, because that is what Francesca chose for me. I have only ever worn clothes that she picked.

—Do you mind?

Caro asks, one day, and I lie and say that of course I don't, because I know that it would upset her to hear the truth, which is that I can't imagine a world in which I had a choice.

—There's nothing wrong with green and blue,

says Sal, whose clothes are brown.

—I think she did it on purpose,

she says to me, when Caro has gone out of the room to find the book that she was reading.

—Francesca. I never wore brown before. It makes me look like potatoes.

Caro's clothes are black.

—Apt,

says Sal, and smiles at me, because she knows that I know how difficult she finds Caro, sometimes, and this is her way of telling me that it is only exasperation. It is not a lack of affection.

ii

Some things I understand by analogy. I am grateful that I can remember the rattle of the train the day that we came to the high house, the way it shook me side to side, the tremble of its machinery underneath my hands on the windowpane, because it means that I have some idea of what it must have been like to be inside a bus, a truck, a boat with more than sails. I wish I could remember more. Sometimes I think that, if I had known what was coming, I could have made more of an effort – but I was only a child and, besides, what difference would it make? Those things are gone, or they are ruined, and we can't rebuild them.

Sally

S PRING promises, but it is not yet here. Dark comes early, and in the evenings we sit close to the kitchen range. Outside, the air is still and it is cold. There will be a hard frost tonight and we have brought the chickens into the scullery. I can hear them scratch and squawk – soft, comfortable noises. Caro has been out running and now she is soaking her feet in a bucket of water. Pauly is mending tools with wire and string. There is less work to do in the garden in the winter, but then we have less energy to do it. We think almost exclusively about keeping warm, and if not that, then we think about being hungry. I am arranging potatoes in the fire to bake. When they are done, we will eat them with salt, and try not to remember how good butter was.

i

Among ourselves – Caro, and Pauly, and I – we don't talk about what we have lost. Loss is such a private thing, and besides, ours is so vast, so absolute, that it is hard to know what we could say, or, if we found a way to start, how we would ever stop – but to myself I make lists. I count the things that I miss, as I stand in the dull winter light, picking slugs off the cabbages: being warm in winter; the clean feeling which comes from using soap. Butter. Coffee. Hot running water from the tap. The routine absence of hunger and worry. Not having to think about the constant eking out of our resources. Lemons. Frozen pizza. Ice cubes. Grandy.

Caro

I MISS the Pauly who was a child. I miss the time when my joints didn't ache, and when my fingers weren't stiff in the morning. I miss being able to sleep. I miss father – not who he was, which I can hardly remember, but the certainty of him, the sense I had that he would stand between me and the world, and that I would be safe. Sometimes, I even miss Francesca.

5

Sally

O N the first Saturday of September I took Pauly into the village, where the post office, shutting for the year, was selling off its last few ice creams cheap. We bought a Cornetto each and sat on the swings, watching the putting-away of things. All around us, paths were being swept. Rugs were being shaken from doorways. Cars were being packed. All the summer visitors were going home, and I found myself thinking of swallows – how they, too, would once have been getting ready to leave, gathering into flocks as soon as September came – tired, suddenly, of summer's stillness.

Pauly was watching a woman strap a child into a car seat, the way she tugged with irritation at the straps to tighten them, tutting as the child wriggled.

—Will they come back?

he asked.

—Will they all come back next year?

At the same moment I heard someone behind me say,

—I don't suppose we'll come again—

A seagull landed on the green. The child in the car seat started to cry. We finished our ice creams.

—Come on, Pauly,

I said.

—Time to go home. Caro will be wondering where we are.

Pauly

S LOWLY, as the village emptied, I expanded the area that was mine. I wandered and explored. It was heaven, for a small boy, to spend all day roaming across the heath or through the marshes, and then to come back to the high house, tired, and sit with Grandy eating piles of bread and jam while Caro, at the stove, said,

—Oh, Pauly, you'll spoil your tea—

Even then, before the flood, this was a landscape which had been both made and lost. There were the windmills, the embankments and the ditches, the reeds, once grown for weaving, now run wild. They would die back in the winter, Grandy told me, but in the spring new growth like spears would come up through the remnants of the old. He said they could be used to make nets and ropes, matting for floors – even roofs, if necessary. He told me about the trees which grew up on the heath, away from the sea, the coppiced oaks that made strange shapes, their trunks split low to form broad bowls, and how once a single branch would be tended for eighty years to make a ship's mast. For the best part of a century, he said, they had been left alone, and now they were just smudged ghosts of their intended shapes.

—I like to climb them,

I said. He smiled, and ruffled my hair with his hand.

—Well, they're very good for climbing. An unintended consequence.

Sometimes, in the afternoons, Sally took me to the church, where I would stand, staring up at the roof, at the wooden angels, wordless and wonderful, the paint fading from their wings, their watchful faces. All these things were new, once, and done with purpose – and all around me I could feel how the land was haunted by them, as now it is haunted again, by the ruins of the village, by the rusting bodies of cars and the cornfields gone to seed, and by the boats which we see floating offshore, sometimes, drifting on the currents out at sea.

i

Sometime during the summer, a pair of great egrets had made their nest in the reed beds. I found them by accident one day and, overjoyed, ran tumbling back to the high house to tell Grandy.

—We are lucky indeed,

he said.

—They must have thought us very special.

ii

As our lives narrowed, as it became only the four of us, with not even the strangers in the village to give the illusion that we belonged to anything beyond ourselves, the two birds became my companions – imaginary friends that my faith, my longing had made real. The others were often busy. I had the impression of things going on in the house which I could neither see nor understand – conversations which took place beyond my hearing – and so I searched for a comforter and I found the pair of ghost birds, tall and beautiful in the marshes. I thought about them constantly, and drew pictures of them in a notebook I had found in the barn and kept, secret, underneath my pillow, and as often as I could, all through the early autumn, I went to visit them. I went alone, or with Caro if she would come, holding hands as we walked along the duckboard paths, the reeds tall on either side, growing up through mud and brackish water. Between the reeds, cut into the earth at intervals, were channels, ditches kept clear for irrigation or as a place for the sea to run when the tides were high, and every so often the shell of a windmill rose, rotted sails hanging above doors which gaped, open and empty. It was, and remains, a place of many birds. Often, turning a corner in the path, Caro and I would see swans, in pairs or threes, making their slow processions, and there were the long-beaked curlews who called out in the evening, and the herons, standing in the water watching, one leg tucked in high under their breasts. There were dunlin and sanderlings, redshanks, snipe. There were the oystercatchers which I loved for their cheerfulness, their black-and-white feathers and their bright beaks and, further up the beach where the cliffs rose above the sea, sand martins, diving and swooping.

iii

The place where the egrets nested was in the very centre of the marsh and it took Caro and me an hour to walk there. We went slowly, because I liked to poke around in the soft mud wherever I was able, looking for grubs or beetles, worms, woodlice. It was good to be the two of us together, away from the others.

—I love you, Caro,

I said. She squeezed my hand.

—I love you too.

When we got close to the nest, I made her stop and stay very still, both of us crouching in the mud until one or other of the birds rose, white and tall – a ghost heron, stalking towards the water. When it was late in the afternoon, and the sun was low and made the water burn gold with its reflection, the birds seemed to be illuminated, gilded at their edges like the angels in the church roof – and I was sure, then, that they possessed the power of protection. Grandy had told me that egrets like these didn't really belong on our marsh but lived, ordinarily, much further south, and so it seemed sensible to me to believe that they must have come with some purpose – that they must have come, somehow, for me.

Sally

WITH the end of summer, a change came. It had been easy, all through the long holiday weeks, to believe that the high house was a kind of paradise, with everything we could ever want stored for us in the barn and nothing to do except keep the garden, or wander to the beach and back – but now the evenings began to darken, the sky inking up while we were still putting Pauly to bed, and still there was no rain. The hedges were dusty. Grass died. The leaves on the trees neither reddened nor dropped but instead began to brown and curl, and they clung to their branches so that when the wind blew, they rattled. In the evenings, when the others were in bed, I started watching the news again. There were cities in the southern hemisphere where they had run out of water, their reservoirs dried by two decades of drought. I saw videos of the trucks which brought rations in from outside, the queues of people waiting with their five-gallon tanks, the lines of soldiers standing guard. The heat was everywhere, and the drought, and down past the marshes, at the beach, the salt sea was climbing onto the land.

i

Grandy and I stood in the orchard, where the apples, swollen with sunshine, hung from the branches, even while the leaves turned brown.

—There is no word for this,

he said.

—There is no word for whatever this season is which comes, these days, between summer and autumn. I am very tired of waiting.

His arm was linked through mine, and I felt the weight of him, how he leaned into me, relying on me for balance.

—We all are,

I said, and wondered why tears rose up to prick my eyes.

ii

I found that I couldn't bear, any longer, to be still. Everything annoyed me. The house annoyed me – its untidiness, the things which were out of place, put down carelessly on a window ledge and not picked up again, the odd socks scrunched in corners, the layer of grease on the high shelves in the kitchen. Caro annoyed me, how apologetic she was.

—Is there anything I can do to help?

she asked, as I knelt on the kitchen floor, surrounded by tins, my head in the cupboard I was trying to clean.

—Jesus, Caro,

I snapped.

—Just pick something and do it, okay? You don't need me to give you instructions.

Pauly, asking me questions, asking for snacks, annoyed me. The chickens annoyed me. Even Grandy annoyed me.

—That chair is disgusting,

I said, as he sat by the open doors in the kitchen.

—Sit somewhere else for once and I'll clean it.

He smiled.

—This is a black mood, Sal—

but I only scowled, and ran water into a bowl to start scrubbing his chair.

iii

In the evenings, in darkness, after the others were in bed, I sat at the bottom of the stairs, my fists balled against my eyelids, exhausted, overwrought, but too afraid to call a halt to the day because I knew that, lying in bed, waiting for sleep, would be when the desolation came, and the thought of all the people – all those who, elsewhere, were dying, from hunger or drought, fire or wind or frost, while I, in my sanctuary, scrubbed out my anger against the floorboards with soap and water.

Caro

T HE last few weeks before the weather broke, I felt that I was living in a headache. The sky seemed to press on me, squeezing my body into a smaller and smaller space, and the light, which for a month had glowed, illuminating each tired branch, each exhausted blade of grass, had taken on a sick, yellow tinge. I stayed indoors. I had started reading *The Lion, the Witch and the Wardrobe* to Pauly and now he was engrossed in it and we had begun on the rest of the series, reading in bed in the morning, and then after breakfast in the living room, me lying on the sofa with my feet crossed on its arm, Pauly on the floor building houses out of Lego.

—Can we go and see my birds this afternoon?

he asked at lunch.

—Let's finish our chapter first,

I said, and because I was enjoying reading the books as much as he was enjoying listening to them, we stayed as we were for the rest of the afternoon, and the next day the same. Even Sal stayed close to the house, and Grandy stayed in the kitchen. They both seemed restless. Grandy sat by the window, staring through it as though he were watching for something, and Sally, who was in a filthy temper, had begun to make an inventory of the house, and to clean, sweeping the floors, turning the mattresses and airing the beds, scrubbing the sinks.

—You'll be putting us in the compost next,

I said, but she didn't smile. She only went on unpacking all the winter blankets from their chest to check for moth.

Sally

F OR days I stayed close to the house, some instinct making me cling, but at last I couldn't bear it any longer.

—I'm going for a swim,

I said, and went out before anyone could try and join me. That was the last afternoon before the rain, and, lying on my back in the sea, feeling its rising and falling, feeling my muscles unclench, I got stung by a jellyfish and had to walk back to the high house with red welts across my shoulders and my arms, trying not to cry. When I got there, Grandy picked pieces of tentacle from my skin with tweezers.

—You need to hold it in hot water,

he said when he was done,

—as hot as you can stand,

and he emptied the kettle into the washing-up bowl. I picked it up, furious with myself and with the jellyfish, and with Grandy for what I saw as his lack of sympathy.

—I'm going to sit outside,

I said. Caro followed me, although I didn't want her to.

—Where's Pauly?

I asked.

—Playing with his Lego,

she answered.

—He was worried about you, but I told him that you're fine. He wants you to go and see him before he goes to bed.

Grandy came outside to join us.

—The weather's changing,

he said, and as he spoke I felt it: a chill, the temperature dropping from one moment to the next as though a switch had been turned. The wind blew the smell of the sea into the garden. We picked up our things, and we went back into the house.

i

Caro gave Pauly his bath and put him to bed while I stoked the fire in the range. The cold was a shock, after so many months, and our skin puckered at the feel of it. Grandy went to bed early but Caro and I, unwilling to leave the warmth of the kitchen, stayed up, playing Uno, waiting. Then, at last, we heard it – the rain, its first few drops tapping against the windows, pattering on the scullery roof, and I had forgotten how it could be – the soft sound of its starting, its steadfastness or constancy, the way it could clean and comfort. We wrapped ourselves in blankets and went to stand by the open kitchen doors, the lights off so that we could see out, and we watched it, falling steadily through the dark. It was a joy like the joy of reunion and I hadn't realised, until then, quite how much I had been longing for it – the end of the summer; the closing of the year; the rain.

Pauly had come downstairs without our noticing, while Caro and I had been shoulder to shoulder staring out into the garden, and now he stood in the middle of the kitchen floor, crying. He held a pillow in his hand, the sleeves of his pyjamas reaching to his knuckles, his hair ruffled, his face pink from sleep. He always seemed younger in the night, I thought, than he did in the day. Caro went to him, knelt down, put her arms around him.

—Pauly,

she said, as he continued to sob.

—Pauly, what's wrong? Did the noise wake you? It's only the rain, Pauly. It's just rain—

—My birds, Caro,

he cried, his voice distorted by tears,

—my birds will get wet.

Caro

PAULY came downstairs after the rain started, and he was frightened for his birds. I went to comfort him and found that his hands and feet were icy.

—He's cold,

I said to Sal.

—Oh, Pauly, you're freezing. Come on, I'll take you back to bed.

I got in beside him and curled my body to his, pulling the duvet over us. Sally came up with blankets which she had fetched from the chest, and jumpers from the barn, and thick socks. I spread one of the blankets out on top of Pauly's bed, and then another one.

—Do we have hot water bottles?

I asked.

—I don't know,

Sally answered.

—I expect so, but it's too dark to look properly now. I'll see what I can do tomorrow.

She said goodnight, and I heard her go downstairs, and then, a little while later, come back up on the way to her own room. I lay in the dark and listened to Pauly's breathing evening out, stretching as he fell asleep again, and I listened to the rain, the drumming of it on the window and the soft roar which was the sound of the wind and the sea. I thought that there were words in it, hidden deep, and I tried to understand what they were but couldn't, and then I slept and didn't wake until the morning, when the smell of wet earth was like a prayer of thanksgiving.

Sally

W E ate breakfast watching the rain run down the out-
sides of the windowpanes. Pauly begged Caro to take
him to see his birds.

—What if they're too wet, Caro?

he said.

—What if their nest has been swept away?

I said,

—They're birds, Pauly. They'll cope,

which earned me a sharp look from Grandy, because of
course they were not just birds to Pauly, which all of us knew.
To make up for it, I said,

—Oh, all right. If Caro doesn't want to go, I'll take you.

He smiled, and jumped up straight away, running towards
the hallway.

—But if your feet get wet,

I called after him,

—you'll just have to put up with it. I'm not carrying you
home because you have damp socks.

i

It was a joy that day to be out in the rain. Pauly and I wore waxed coats and trousers from the barn, and wellington boots, and we had gloves on our hands and hats and scarves under our hoods, so that we were warm and dry despite the weather, and as we walked down past the tide pool to the marshes we splashed in puddles and we slipped in mud and we sang, loudly, our voices swallowed up by the constant drumming of water on earth. We played chasing games. On the duckboard paths we picked our way carefully because the wood was slippery in places.

—Hold tight to my hand,

I said to Pauly.

—I don't want to lose you. What would Caro say?

The birds were still in their nest, although when we saw the larger of the pair rise to strut towards the channel and stand at its edge, one leg delicately raised as though to keep it clear of the mud, he looked bedraggled, his feathers flattened. He dipped his head low to peer at the water. We watched him, crouching on the path, until suddenly his beak shot forward, his neck extending in one swift, smooth movement to pierce the rain-pocked surface of the water and fetch out a fish which thrashed its silver tail and then was gone, swallowed up into the bird's long throat.

—Well, that's good, Pauly, isn't it?

I said.

—You know he's had his tea. Come on. We should be getting back.

Halfway home, Pauly pulled on my arm and I bent low so that I could hear what he was saying through the sound of the rain on my hood.

—My feet are a little bit wet, Sal,

he said,

—but I don't mind,

and he smiled, and ran off, ahead of me, towards the house.

Caro

E VERY afternoon now Pauly wanted to see his birds, and
so we took him, Sally or I, walking through soft rain
or through torrents, or through the mist which rolled in, at
times, from the sea. On days when the weather was very bad,
when the wind blew the rain into sharp points which stung the
exposed skin of my face, bringing tears to my eyes, or when the
temperature dropped and turned the rain to sleet, I suggested
to Pauly that perhaps we might leave the birds for a day.

—They'll be hiding, Pauly. They'll be in their nest in weather
like this. We won't see them,

but the thought seemed to terrify him.

—They're frightened, Caro. I know they are,

and so we went.

—I don't know how long they'll last,

Grandy said one night, after Pauly had gone to bed.

—They should have flown south months ago, but the
weather's fooled them. Now they're stuck. They can't make
the journey in all this rain. You'll have to prepare him, Caro—

and I knew that he was right, but still I didn't do it. I found
I couldn't bear the thought of Pauly's fear, or of his grief, this
new grief, and so I put it off, saying nothing one day and

then nothing the next, and, miraculously, the birds clung on, thinner and more pitiful every time we saw them, but still alive, all through the last weeks of November and into the start of December.

i

The rain was a constancy but there were variations in it. Sometimes it was a fine mist, a falling mist that lay in drops on hair and clothes like tiny jewels, and at others it was a steady pouring which found its way inside zips and seams. There were days when the wind blew it into daggers that stung our hands, our faces. There were days when it was nothing more than a never-ending background of wet and grey, and even, once, an afternoon when I stood on the embankment by the river and watched the clouds part, out at sea, to let a shaft of sunlight through which split and glittered and made a rainbow over the heath. Mostly it was only rain. We grew used to being sodden. Our clothes, left to dry on the rail of the kitchen range, filled the house with steam. Our boots began to smell of mould and of the rotting of the glue which held the uppers and the soles together. I got used to pulling on gloves which were still damp, forcing my fingers into them, my thumbs. My skin, saturated, began to soften and to split in weals along the sides of my palms.

Sally

T HE rain went on, and I began to think that this was what
we had been preparing for – and how I congratulated
myself, each time I unblocked a gutter or a drain, on our resil-
ience. I put on my wellingtons and Grandy's old sou'wester and
went out to check the garden, to pick the last of the autumn
raspberries, to pull the leaves of the perpetual spinach. I let
the chickens out to scratch in the wet earth and then called
them back into the scullery, and I thought how fine it was
to be so well prepared. I didn't think about the supermarket
vans which still came monthly. I didn't think about the things
we used but couldn't make: the sugar, the milk, the bottles of
olive oil. I didn't think about the doctors and the hospitals
who would be there if we wanted them. I didn't think about
all the mechanical things, the fridge and the generator, the
lights with their bulbs, the taps which turned. I didn't think
about that vast net which, invisible, imperceptible, held us up.

i

It was easy to believe, all through those long grey weeks of rain,
that we were already the only ones left in the universe, but in

truth I think I could still feel them – the others; the cities and the towns of people who went about their business as usual, finding their small familiar joys and telling one another that, after all, it was the best they could do. The rain fell on all of us. It drenched us the same, and in the weeks and months after the flood, that is what was lost: that sense of being a small part of a whole which persisted, even when we might dislike everything about it. Afterwards, all that was left were fragments: people who clung on, as we did. We saw them. They came often, in those first few weeks, to see what had happened to the village. Perhaps they thought it would be a safe place to stay. All the news was of the cities which had been hit, and the only way to find out about places like this was to see for oneself. Pauly had a pair of binoculars that Grandy had given him for Christmas, and we used them to watch, hiding in the trees between the village and the high house. They came to the edge of the water to stand, looking – and then, after what might be five minutes or thirty, they went away again, back the way they had come, towards the road.

—They've gone!

Pauly called, and Caro and I came out from where we were hiding and carried on picking over the village. We were looking for anything we could salvage – things that had been stored above the water level, in attics or on the higher floors, clothes in particular, blankets, sewing kits. We took the light bulbs out of their sockets. We hunted through drawers looking for batteries, for wire, for pairs of scissors. We took an axe to any wooden furniture we could find and carried it out as firewood. Caro hated it. All the way through, she kept her mouth tightly shut. She went into rooms quickly and left as soon as she could. She complained of headaches. She went to bed early, but in the morning her face would be pale, her eyes dark, and so I knew she didn't sleep.

ii

Now it is very rare that we see anybody. Sometimes there are boats, small yachts or dinghies, their sails sharp against the sky. Sometimes, when I am at the field on the other side of the heath, the one which we use because it is above the flood line, even when the water has been at its highest, so that its earth is not saturated with salt, I see them in the distance, small groups walking slowly along the road. Once, there was a helicopter. There have been planes, although not for years. At the beginning, we feared raiders, but I think Francesca hid us well. She told no one her plans, not even us, and we are on the way to nowhere but the sea. The house cannot be seen from the road. I think there are parts of the world which have fared better than others – or, rather, there are parts of the world where the people are still waiting. They will not come for us – because if they did, then where would be the end of it? They have only so much, and it is not as simple as letting everyone in.

Caro

W E are not self-sufficient. There is no such thing. We rely on the stores we have left in the barn. We rely on the chickens, but the flock is shrinking. We rely on the wheat, but one bad year and we will have none left to sow as seed. We rely on the tide pool and the generator which we cannot fix if it breaks. We rely on the high house, on its fabric, on its shelter and protection, but these things will not last forever. We rely on one another. I try not to be afraid, but I am.

Pauly

WHEN Caro wakes me up in the night, when she says that her mind is so full she cannot bear to think, and needs me to tell her that she isn't to blame, or is no more to blame than the rest of us – when she lies on the mattress on the floor and I whisper stories to her before she falls asleep holding my hand and I see her body soft at last, relaxed – then I weigh up the balance of probabilities. All three of us are in tolerably good health, except for Caro's chilblains, which we treat very carefully so that they don't become infected. We have a small store of antibiotics in the barn, but we save them for emergencies. We have boxes and boxes of paracetamol and ibuprofen. We have one box which contains twenty-one small vials of morphine, and three empty slots. We live in fear of accidents – the missed step, the lost footing. A broken bone, even a small one, would bring serious risk, and we guard ourselves against them with a mixture of protective clothing and superstition. We treat tools with reverence. We sharpen blades carefully, and wear gloves. Even so, it seems probable that each of our futures will contain some degree of extraordinary pain.

Sometimes I think of leaving, but where would I go that would be better than here?

Sally

D ECEMBER came and it had been raining, now, for six weeks. The roads had flooded. We had eaten the last of the butter, drunk the last of the milk. More and more, we were forced to rely on the tide pool for electricity, for the hour or so in every six that it could keep the lights on. The rest of the time we lit candles or stoked the fire to a blaze and it was still, then, exciting, the feeling of being beleaguered, of crouching together for warmth. The last time the post came, it brought a leaflet which warned against taking refuge in roof spaces in the event of floods. I thought of drowning with my face pressed against rafters, unreachable sky on the other side of tiles. I thought of the threat of death by exposure, balanced on the ridge of a pitched roof in wet clothes. I thought of children, waiting for rescue, their bodies already half under the water. The rain went on and the rivers rose and rose. In the city, the barrier which stopped the tide from flooding up into its easterly districts, which was designed to be closed only under extraordinary circumstances, was now shut permanently, a de facto dam, millions of lives held in balance by its bright metal sails. Those downriver of it, on the edges of the long estuary, were evacuated. Those with no alternative were sent to rest centres, compounds in the middle of the country, on the rolling shoulders of the high ridge. They were given tents, and I imagined trying to peg the canvas into the sodden ground. I watched their faces, filmed through wire fences. They sat, hunched into anoraks. They sat as though they had lost the will to do anything else, or as though there was nothing else to be done – which, I suppose, there wasn't. I remembered Grandy telling me, when I was a child and he knelt in front of me, doing up the zip of my snowsuit, that the important thing in wet weather is not to let the rain in, because once you are wet it is so hard to get dry again, and I thought of being wet all the time. There were rumours of archaic diseases: trench foot, dysentery, cholera.

i

Beside the threat of water, there was the threat of hunger. Farm animals floated, drowned, in flooded fields. The earth was too wet to yield a crop. Ports, inundated, evacuated, struggled to give harbour to those few container ships which still came. The whole complicated system of modernity which had held us up, away from the earth, was crumbling, and we were becoming again what we had used to be: cold, and frightened of the weather, and frightened of the dark. Somehow, while we had all been busy, while we had been doing those small things which added up to living, the future had slipped into the present – and, despite the fact that we had known that it would come, the overwhelming feeling, now that it was here, was of surprise, like waking up one morning to find that you had been young, and now, all at once, you weren't. I saw what was happening, and my safety sat on me like a weight, but there was Pauly to think of, and Caro, and Grandy. We only had enough for ourselves.

ii

Caro went out running and came home to tell us that our own river, up beyond the bridge, had burst its banks and lay in silver sheets across the fields, and still – still – despite all I saw and knew, I told myself that perhaps it was only another bad year. Something would happen, or something would be done, to keep everyone safe. It was, I think, a form of self-protection, the way my mind slipped off the truth. It was a way of keeping us safe. Caro couldn't do it. She was like Francesca in that respect, the year that I had known her, but without Francesca's pragmatism, her countermanding rage – or only, perhaps, without the advantage of having been born sooner, and freer. She couldn't tune out the suffering of other people, or think that someone else must be responsible for them. She couldn't weigh the costs and find an answer, but could only see how gross the injustice was – us in the high house, dry, while all across the country people waited in the rain. One night, she came into my room and sat next to me on my bed, watching on my laptop, and afterwards she was inconsolable. We should, she said, fill up the bedrooms. We should open our gates. We should let them come, anyone who needed to, into the high house, into the dry – I held her, the first time I had ever done so, and the last, and I told her it wasn't possible. I told her the truth: that we couldn't save ourselves and them as well – and anyway, out of all those people, all those desperate hundreds, who should we choose, and how? There wasn't room for everyone. And if, later, it became a choice between them and Pauly, what would we do then? She refused to answer my questions and I, in turn, began to keep the news away from her.

iii

—Pauly,

I said,

—this is important. If you are up on the heath and you see anyone, you need to hide, okay? And if anyone asks you, say you're from the town. Don't tell them about the high house. He nodded his head, and went on tying bits of twig together with string to make a raft.

iv

In the end, it was my decision, because no one else would make it. I saw those thousands and thousands of faces, those multitudes of hopeless people in their rain-soaked clothes, the mud streaked through their hair, and I decided that Pauly was more important, and Caro, too, because she was also in my care. That is what I did. I could have let them come, even just one or two of them. I could have decided that, perhaps, with more people, we would have found a way to live, and that what we had was only a starting point – but what if, in a year's time, we had built nothing, and had nothing? What if too many came, and we were overwhelmed? I had to draw a line, and so I drew it, and Pauly is still alive, and so is Caro, and so am I.

Caro

PAULY had his birds, and Sally had the stores and the garden, and I ran. These were the things that we thought about because we couldn't think about what was happening. I don't know about Grandy. Sally would say he thought about us, and how much there was left to teach us, and perhaps that's true. It seemed to me that since the rain had started, he had begun to get slower, and I wondered if the cold and the damp made his joints ache. Sally had put his chair by the range in the kitchen and now he rarely moved from it. He sat with a blanket over his knees and watched us as we came and went. Sometimes he read to Pauly. Sometimes he told Pauly stories. Pauly sat on the floor with his back against Grandy's legs, and his feet in their socks which never matched slid up against the range.

—Careful, Pauly,

I said,

—or your feet will catch fire.

I didn't want Pauly to love Grandy so much. I laced up my shoes, and went out to run.

i

I ran in the early morning, when dawn came slow behind the clouds. I ran in the afternoon, when everything was dull and grey. I ran along the familiar paths, across the heath, through the empty village, through the reed beds down to the sea, where the waves turned and turned and beat against the beach, and as long as I was running, I was not afraid.

ii

I ran in the dark, after Pauly was in bed. I carried a wind-up torch and ran into the bright circle that it made. The rain, falling through the torch beam, shone, each droplet bright, and that was the world: the small area of light, the rain caught in it, my feet in the darkness. I ran to the sea and found that it was different at night. It was larger and louder and it was not water, or shore, or spray or waves. It was one entity, vast and singular, whose voice was a roar, who was not still, whose mind was not on us. I felt how cold it was. I felt the rivers which bled into its tall waves, the currents that they made. I smelt the seaweed which rotted on the beach, that Grandy made us carry home to spread on the potato beds. I heard a bird say *pee-wit*.

iii

I run the same paths, now, and each time, as I circle back on myself, running up past the tide pool, through the hedge, across the orchard to the kitchen door, I feel I have got free of something. I feel I am better, at last, and I think how wonderful it will be to walk into the warm kitchen and be so easy in myself. I think how much it will please Sally, and how it will change things for Pauly – but it never lasts. I cross the barrier from dark to light, from rain to dry, and feel myself fold in again. I feel anxiety creep back, and grief, and guilt.

Sally

I T was a few days before Christmas, and Pauly and Caro and I were in the kitchen with Grandy, making pastry for mince pies with suet instead of butter because we had no butter left, now that the vans weren't coming out from the town any more. We kneaded it and rolled it out, and I gave Pauly a glass to cut it with.

—Do I like mince pies?

he asked, and Caro answered,

—I'm not sure anyone likes mince pies really. Definitely not these ones—

The doorbell rang, making us all jump. Pauly rubbed his floury hands down his sweater and ran towards the door. I said,

—I didn't even know we had a doorbell.

Grandy shrugged.

—Best go and see,

he said, and so I followed Pauly, who had reached the front door but was still, then, just too short to undo the catch.

—There's someone there, Sally,

he said,

—Who is it?

—Oh, Pauly, how would I know?

and I opened the door to find the vicar standing there, a sort of hooded rain cape flapping over his clerical suit.

—Good lord,

I said,

—it's you.

He smiled.

—Not quite—

and then,

—This is rotten weather indeed.

—I'm sorry. Of course. Come in.

I stepped to one side and let him past, and Pauly led the way back into the kitchen where Caro stood, her arms crossed, with her back to the table.

—Caro,

I told her,

—this is the vicar. From the church in the village. He's an old friend of Grandy's.

She didn't answer. I watched her face tighten.

—Pleased to meet you,

the vicar said.

—I was so sorry to hear about your parents. It must be a terrible loss—

—My father,

Caro interrupted.

—Francesca wasn't my mother. Only Pauly's.

The vicar nodded.

—Still,

he said,

—in some ways that can make things harder, can't it?

Caro didn't answer. He turned to Grandy.

—It's been a long time, friend.

Grandy smiled.

—I find that I am too old, now, for churches,

he said,

—but I must say that I am pleased to see you.

i

Company turned the evening into a party. I made a pot of vegetable soup with barley in it, and we ate at the kitchen table, and afterwards there were the mince pies. Everyone except Pauly was too kind to say that they were horrible.

—I don't like it,

Pauly said.

—I thought I would, but I don't. Can I have something else?

and I went to fetch him a small box of chocolates that I had bought from the village shop before it closed and had hidden, half-forgotten, in my sock drawer.

—Well, this has been a rare treat,

the vicar said, when we had finished, and the dishes had been cleared away,

—but I'm afraid I have not come entirely without a cause in mind.

Grandy looked at him.

—Now we come to it,

he said, as though addressing all of us, and the two men smiled at one another.

—A decision has been made,

the vicar said, leaning back in his chair,

—that the church here is not viable. People still come, of course. Pilgrims. Not many, but the feeling is that we should not be encouraging them.

—They're closing the church,

I said. He shrugged.

—It is a temporary measure, I am told. Until the winter is over—

—But who knows,

Grandy said,

—when this winter will be over.

—In spring, I would have thought,

the vicar said, with some asperity.

—Regardless,

he went on,

—I will hold one last service. I am old—

Grandy snorted—

—I am old, and sentimental. Christmas morning, I thought. I would like to have the sun rise on us.

—You're asking us to come?

—I am asking you to come.

Pauly, his face covered with chocolate, said,

—Will you pray for my birds?

—Your birds?

—A pair of great egrets,

I explained.

—They're nesting out on the marshes. The weather seems to have confused them and they're trying to overwinter here. Pauly goes to visit them every day, to make sure that they're safe.

—Well,

the vicar said,

—I don't see why not. Who needs our prayers, if not the birds?

ii

Early in the afternoon of Christmas Eve, Pauly and I walked down to the marshes.

—It's not that I don't love you,

Pauly had said to me, when I told him it was my turn to take him.

—It's only that Caro is better. For this. Not for everything.

—Sorry, Pauly,

Caro said,

—I've got Christmas business—

because she was to spend the afternoon in the barn, choosing things from the stores to give to Pauly for his Christmas presents, and wrapping them up in salvaged tissue paper on which, I found when we got back, she had drawn hundreds of tiny stars.

iii

The water, I noticed, as we made our way to the place where the egrets had their nest, was almost up to the edge of the path now, and the boards were very slippery and were spread with seaweed in places, but I didn't think anything of it.

—We *TISS*ue a merry Christmas,

Pauly sang, and his voice was so filled with joy that there was no room left in the world for anything else. I ignored the water, and thought instead what a strange thing it was, to have Christmas in the high house, and to feel, despite everything, such love, such happiness – and I thought how, whatever might happen, I could not regret how Caro had come, and brought Pauly with her.

iv

—Birds, birds, birds,

Pauly whispered, crouching down close to the nest,

—birds, birds, birds – it's Christmas tomorrow, birds. You're going to be safe.

—Time to go, Pauly,

I said.

—My hands are cold.

v

—If god was anything,

Pauly remarked, as he sat in a large bucket by the fire in the kitchen, letting Caro pour pans of hot water over his head to wash his hair,

—then he would be a lion.

—I would have thought,

I said,

—that you would choose a bird.

—Not a bird.

—Not even an eagle?

Pauly looked at me as though he thought me stupid.

—Of course not,

he said.

—A lion.

vi

Pauly unwrapped his new pyjamas and, dried from his bath, put them on. I made everyone hot chocolate with powdered milk and water.

—A very merry Christmas,

Grandy said – and if I could give back everything that came afterwards to have, in exchange for it, that afternoon again – to have the sound of Pauly's singing, to have Caro's stars, and Grandy – then I think, perhaps, I might.

Pauly

I T was Grandy who had explained to me about prayer, one afternoon when I had been asking him about the church, and what it had been made for.

—It is a way of talking to god,

he said.

—If you believe in that sort of thing. Which some do, and some don't.

—Do you?

I asked.

—I am an old man,

he answered.

—I hedge my bets. But it has been a long time since I went inside the church.

Now, getting ready for bed, putting on my new pyjamas by the fire, I imagined how it would be the next morning – how all four of us and the vicar would stand in the church, our heads bowed and our hands folded – and how, to answer us, a lion would come, bounding in with the dawn, its huge paws beating the air. I imagined it stopping on the boards, out beyond the village where the birds were nesting. I imagined it raising its gold head to sniff before it picked its way through the reeds – and then, when it had found the place, I imagined how it would take the birds into its soft mouth and, turning, rising, would carry them away, south, for the winter.

Sally

W E stood in the dark hallway of the high house, early on Christmas morning, wrapped up in our jumpers and our scarves, our hats and gloves.

—I don't want to wear my coat,

Pauly said.

—It'll be cold in the church,

I told him,

—the heating hasn't been on for weeks.

—Can you carry it, then?

—No.

—Caro, will you carry it? Please?

but Caro wasn't listening. She looked pale, and stood a little apart from us, staring out of the window at the darkness through which the rain continued to fall.

—I think it's getting heavier again,

she said, and Grandy answered,

—Not long now.

We waited until the vicar came, a black crow under a large umbrella, to hammer on the door, and then we followed him out, and we must have made a small and ragtag processional, if anyone could have seen us – walking slowly, one after the other, down the path towards the gate. The vicar had brought his car and we clambered into it, Grandy in the front with his stick between his knees, and Caro and I on either side in the back with Pauly sandwiched in the middle. The heater was on and the smell of it was like nothing except the smell a car heater makes inside a car on a dark, wet morning, which was the smell of a world already lost to us. We breathed it in. Somewhere, beyond the thick cloud which wrapped the earth, beyond the cloud which spilled its water down to swell the rivers, to fill the sea, the sky must have been starting to lighten, but it was impossible to tell.

—Seat belts on?

the vicar asked, and he started the engine, and we drove off towards the church.

i

—Caro, Caro, I feel sick,

Pauly said. The car rocked about on the rough lane towards the bridge.

—Does he get carsick?

I asked.

—I don't know,

Caro answered.

—It's been so long since we were in a car. He wasn't last time.

—It'll be the warmth,

the vicar said,

—it always makes me feel a bit off when I'm in the back.

Especially when it's dark. Here, Paul. Be sick into this if you need to.

He passed back a plastic bag and I held it over Pauly's lap for the rest of the journey, although in the end he wasn't sick after all – and then we were there, parked in the road beside the churchyard wall, and it was all so very ordinary, and so strange. We got out of the car and walked through the lychgate, past the leafless apple tree, the grass which Grandy hadn't mown all year. I wondered who else had done it, because it was long but not a meadow. We reached the church's porch, the heavy door. The vicar opened it.

—Go in,

he said,

—and I'll be with you shortly—

and, pausing with his hand on the latch, he added,

—Thank you.

We went into the church, and up the nave. The light was grey now, sunrise getting nearer, and there were the angels in the rafters, their faces peering from the shadows, an ancient and familiar congregation. I watched Caro, her hands in her pockets, walk up towards the altar and slip into a pew, and Grandy showing Pauly the place where, on the base of the font, a mouse had been carved, and a cat to chase it. I saw the scorch marks where three-hundred-year-old lightning had run down to earth through the iron rivets of the thick oak door, and felt beneath my feet the dished stone of the flags. There was the smell of incense, and the cold. I went into my own accustomed spot and, for all my unbelief, I knelt, and closed my eyes.

ii

Sometime during the service the sun rose, but we couldn't see it. The rain was a constant torrent and the wind, blowing steadily in from the sea, threw it against the clear glass of the chancel window.

—Almighty God,

the vicar said,

—who hast given us thy only begotten Son, grant that we being regenerate, and made thy children by adoption and grace, may daily be renewed by thy Holy Spirit—

—It doesn't seem likely,

Grandy muttered, under his breath.

iii

We drove back to the high house and, now that it was light, we saw, as we crossed the bridge, how swollen the river was, running brown and fast and already almost up to the top of the embankment.

—Full moon tomorrow,

Grandy said.

—Spring tide. And the wind behind it, too, unless it drops or turns,

and I thought, for a moment, of the seaweed spread up across the paths over the marshes, but we were in a party mood, and I didn't want to spoil it. The water could wait, I thought, and we sang 'Good King Wenceslas' with the vicar taking the part of the king and Caro and me trilling along as the page.

We sang 'Once in Royal David's City' and 'O Little Town of Bethlehem'. We sang 'God Rest You Merry, Gentlemen' and, because we had forgotten the words, we took it in turns to make them up. We sang 'Hark! The Herald Angels Sing' and Caro, her voice surprisingly beautiful, high and clear, provided the descant.

—I learned it at school,

she said, and shrugged, embarrassed by our praise.

When we got back to the high house we piled out of the car and in through the front door and it was warm and welcoming, and we turned on the lights, which were working.

—A Christmas miracle,

Grandy said. We went into the kitchen and while I stoked the fire in the range, and lit another in the stove, Caro made drop scones. Pauly cracked the eggs.

—Try not to get so much shell in this time, Pauly,

but a piece got in anyway, and when it turned up in the vicar's breakfast we laughed and told him it was lucky.

—I haven't had a Christmas morning like this in years,

he said.

—I'm normally so busy,

and he sat back in his chair and smiled at us. Caro said,

—Stay with us. You could stay with us. You could live here.

She caught my eye.

—What? He could, Sal. It's my house, after all,

and I shrugged.

—Thank you,

the vicar said, looking, suddenly, very tired, so that I wondered for the first time where he had been staying, and what he had been doing, in those long months since I had last seen him,

—that is a very generous offer indeed, and I am grateful, but it would not, I think, be sensible. Besides, I fear that I will soon be needed elsewhere.

He stood up.

—It's time that I was off. It has been a tremendous pleasure, and perhaps one day I will come back and you can show me round your garden which is, I am sure, wonderful. I thought that I might leave the key to the church here. There is another with the diocese office, of course, but I think that, as you are closest, you should have this one.

He put the key down on the table, and I thought it looked both too large and too old to have such an ordinary purpose as opening a door. The vicar turned to Caro and said,

—Thank you, again. Your offer was a great kindness. Have courage,

and to Pauly,

—I will keep praying for your birds.

To me he only smiled, and bent his head.

Grandy stood up as well, then, and the two men went together to the front door. I followed them, and watched as, in the hallway, they faced one another. The vicar took Grandy's hand.

—And where is your place, friend?

he asked. Grandy didn't answer.

—I think,

the vicar said,

—that, in such times as these, we might need to adopt a flexible understanding of sin—

—Oh, sin,

Grandy answered.

—Well, I have never had much time for that.

Caro

A FTER lunch on Christmas Day, Pauly said,
—Can we go and see the birds now, Caro?

Outside, the wind blew through the branches of the apple trees so that they shook and bent, and although there were a few hours left before sunset, it was dark enough that it might have been dusk already. The rain fell, fierce and constant.

—Really, Pauly? They'll be all right for one day, surely?

—They won't! Caro, they won't!

Pauly protested, and I gave in.

—You'll have to put two jumpers on,

I said,

—and all your waterproofs.

—I will,

said Pauly,

—and my hat. Two hats!

He ran off to get ready.

i

How much of my life, in those days, did I spend telling Pauly what to wear? And when was the last time? How odd that

such ordinary things should still seem notable, and sad. I miss
his small boy self so powerfully sometimes that it seems to
outweigh everything else – and there it is. A world has ended,
but we have not.

ii

The wind, as we walked down past the tide pool to visit Pauly's
birds, was so strong that we had to lean into it, pushing against
it to walk.

—I'm afraid you'll be blown away,

I called to Pauly, but my voice was swallowed up by the
weather so that he didn't hear. I held his hand tight and it was
the best part of half an hour before we reached the top of the
marshes. My face felt raw from having the rain blown into it,
and my ears ached. When we came to the hedge on the other
side of the copse which separated the high house and the village
from the marsh, we saw that some of the channels through the
reed beds had already burst their banks. Brown water, flecked
through with whitish-yellow foam, swirled across the wooden
path. I knelt down next to Pauly, and said,

—I think we should turn back. There's too much water,
Pauly, we can come again tomorrow,

but he shook his head and, thinking that after all the water
was only an inch over the path, and that it would be easier
to do it quickly than to argue, I let him go, and we carried
on until, not far from the place where the birds' nest must
already have been drowned, I saw ahead of me a wave, and
felt a pull around my ankles, a sudden deepening of the water,

and realised that it wasn't only the flooded marshes that we walked through, swollen by the rain, but the sea itself, come through the shingle bank, and I swung Pauly up in my arms, and turned, and ran.

Pauly

I saw the water swirling over the place where my birds
had lived. I saw that their nest was gone, and I knew for
sure, then, that my prayer had been answered – that the lion
had come, and the birds were saved, and so would we be, too.

Caro

S TILL I didn't realise the extent of it. I suppose it must have been the high tide which had caused the breach, and now it had turned and was ebbing, the water draining back out across the beach. I didn't think what would happen when the tide turned again. I didn't think about the wind which blew in from the sea and would push it, when the time came, higher up onto the land. I didn't think about the moon, which was full. Walls had always held these things at bay before, and, despite everything, it still didn't occur to me that they might not continue to do so. Pauly was soaked from the knees down, water seeping from his boots, and so I carried him back to the high house and thought only how he had grown in the seven months since we had come to the high house, and whether this might be the last time that he let me carry him, and whether he would realise that the egrets were probably dead or whether he would think that they might have escaped – and when we got back I took Pauly's coat off and then my own, and hung them in the scullery where the chickens squawked at the disturbance, and fetched a towel and went and sat down by the fire.

i

—Jesus, Pauly,

    Sally said, holding up one of his boots,

    —how did you manage this? They're soaked.

    —It wasn't his fault,

    I said, but was too ashamed of having let Pauly go out onto the flooded path to tell her any more.

ii

Even now, years later, it terrifies me to think what might have happened if Pauly and I had been an hour earlier, or the tide had turned later, or we hadn't dawdled on the way. I think of the sudden rush of water when the sea broke through. I think how easily Pauly could have slipped, and how I would have lost him. Even now, so long afterwards, when the water has retreated as far as it ever will, when the river has found its new course and settled to it, we find reminders of the flood. On land which has long dried out we see, after wet weather, a rime of salt; and when I dig I find mussel shells, slates, pieces of sea glass, smooth and green, and I crouch in the mud, holding in my hand what I have uncovered, and feel the world tilt towards what might have been.

Sally

I FOUND Pauly's boots, which Caro had left in the scullery. They were filthy, and soaking wet, and so I took them into the kitchen, to put them near the stove to dry. Caro and Pauly were sitting on the hearthrug, wrapped in towels. Grandy had gone into his room to rest.

—Christ,

I said,

—what happened to you?

—We got wet,

she said,

—looking for Pauly's birds. The water is up over the boards on the marshes—

but this happened sometimes, in the winter, after heavy rain, and I didn't think for one moment that she meant the sea had broken through the bank.

i

We sat by the fire and Grandy read us ghost stories. Pauly, exhausted from the long day and from his drenching, fell asleep with his head on Caro's lap. I felt myself get drowsy.

—It's been a long day,

I said.

—Time for bed, I think. Happy Christmas, Grandy. Happy
Christmas, Caro. Do you want any help carrying Pauly up to
bed?

She shook her head.

—I'll let him be for a bit,

she said,

—I'm not quite ready to go up, anyway.

I kissed Grandy, and went upstairs, and crawled into bed,
waiting for the cold sheets to warm, and then I slept.

ii

And when I woke it was to the sound of hammering on my
door and Caro shouting,

—Sally! Sally!

—For Christ's sake,

I shouted back, as I pulled on my trousers,

—what the fuck, Caro? What is it?

It was Grandy who answered.

—The sea has flooded the marshes,

he said.

—The flood is here.

iii

—The sea is up in the village,

   Caro said,

—or it's the river. I can't tell. It's hard to tell.

—How do you know?

I asked.

—I couldn't sleep. I went for a run—

—Jesus Christ, Caro. It's three in the morning. There's a gale.

—It's ten to eleven,

she said, defensiveness making her peevish.

—You went to bed at nine.

—That's enough.

Grandy's voice was sharp, and we were both silent at once.

—There's no time for bickering. High tide is an hour away, maybe a little more. The water won't have peaked yet and even when the tide turns there's no guarantee it will stop rising. We're safe here. Pauly must stay and I will stay with him, but the alarm will have to be sounded.

—Sounded for who?

I asked.

—Everyone's gone. The village is empty. There's no one to hear it, even if we found a way—

—You don't know it's empty,

Caro said,

—there might be someone. What if there's someone and they're sleeping? What if they wake and it's too late already?

She sounded close to tears, and I felt my anger rising to meet her intransigence, because it seemed to me as though, once again, she was passing off the choice to me, forcing me to weigh those costs which she refused to acknowledge.

—And what if you're drowned trying to wake up some non-existent tourists? What do we say to Pauly—

—Take the church key,

Grandy interrupted me, and again his voice silenced us.

—Ring the bell, and keep ringing it. Sal knows how. You can take it in turns. You'll need gloves. And torches.

I opened my mouth to speak, but Grandy took my hand.

—It's not about the village,

he said.

—You're right, but the flood will spread. It won't have reached the town yet, and it'll be moving down the coast, too, with the tide. Ring the bells, and there's a good chance they'll be heard. As quick as you can,

and Caro was putting on her waterproofs, her boots, handing me mine, and I was putting them on, too, even as I said,

—This is fucking stupid,

and I was zipping up my coat, pulling on my hat, taking a torch, because Grandy and Caro were right, and I had only been thinking of us, of the high house, of Pauly.

—Don't take unnecessary risks,

Grandy said,

—but if you can reach the church, ring as long as you can. And if not, you will at least have tried.

I didn't say goodbye. I didn't turn to look back. We were out the door, half running, winding up our torches as we went.

iv

It seemed that there was water everywhere, even before we got to the river and found the flood coming up to meet us.

There was water on the earth and water in the air, and it was in our boots, and in our eyes and mouths. The sound of it filled the dark, and I thought that I could hear the sea, but it was coming from the wrong direction, or it was coming from every direction at once.

v

We stood in the road above the bridge and it was already round our ankles.

—We're too late,

I said to Caro. The water was rising fast, spreading out like a bath filling, and although it seemed, in the beams of our torches, to be quite still, I could feel the pull of it already, the way it sucked and dragged. Caro ignored me, starting to walk down the slope to the start of the bridge. I grabbed her arm, held her. She stopped, but didn't turn her head to look at me. On the other side of the bridge, on the rise of the heath and less than half a mile away, the church stood, a blacker shape against the sky.

—We're too late, Caro,

I said again.

—The water will be up to our waists by the time we get to the middle of the bridge, and god knows what's in it.

I started to shake her arm.

—It's moving too fast. We have to go back, Caro. It's too dangerous. If you fall in, it'll take you. You'll be swept away. For god's sake turn round. Please, Caro.

She shook her head.

—Caro,

I said,

—this is absurd. There's no one to hear the bell. No one will come. Caro, what will Pauly do if you are killed?

—You don't know,

she said.

—You don't know there's no one. We haven't been watching the village. We haven't—

She threw her words across the roar of the flood and I heard the tear in her throat, felt the muscles of her arm harden as she balled her fists tight at her sides—

—There might be someone asleep. There might be someone. There might—

Fear came off her like scent, but it was not fear for us – not even for Pauly. Caro was afraid for everyone, all at once – all those that night who ran or didn't run, who waited through the dark for help which didn't come, who clung to their roofs, who packed their belongings into their cars and drove without a destination – who, all along the coast, were drowned already or were drowning while the rain fell on them as it fell on us, soaking all it touched. It was fear that was compassion, and fear that was rage, and I felt the strength of it, pulling us on. I took her hand, and we waded out, together, onto the bridge.

vi

The water reached our waists and we clung to one another, edging forward step by step. I felt something hit me in the back, a log or plank or piece of fence, perhaps, taking the wind out of me, and for a moment I couldn't stand at all but could only cling to Caro, trying desperately to find the ground with my feet. For a moment – before, miraculously, I felt the tarmacked surface of the bridge again – I knew that I would die, and it was pitiful, to understand what bargains I would have made to live. Caro held on to me.

—Thank you,

I said to her, but my voice was a whisper and the water roared.

vii

For a while, once we were out of the water, I found it easiest to crawl, pushing myself on all fours through gorse and scrub. I had lost my torch, and could do nothing but follow the small circle of light that was made by Caro's, ahead of me, struggling after it until we reached the lychgate, and she pulled me up onto my feet, and felt in my pocket for the church key which Grandy had given me. We walked hand in hand through the church yard, and into the porch. Caro fitted the key into the iron lock and turned it, and finally we were inside, out of the rain, and the noise of the water was behind us.

viii

All night we tolled the church bell. We pulled the rope until our hands blistered, and the blisters split and then bled, until the skin of our palms was raw, and then we pulled again, and the sound of it was a slow beat out across the night. We pulled it until dawn broke, and the sun rose, and then at last we stopped. We climbed up to the top of the tower and looked out across the morning and saw that the rain had finally cleared, the clouds torn to shreds across the new blue sky, and that all the land, those places I had known my whole life, was underneath the water. The village was underneath the water. Only the roofs showed, shining in the sunlight. The beach was gone, and the marsh. The water lay on the fields. And in the whole of it nothing moved but ourselves.

ix

We were too exhausted to make our way back to the high house and so we lay, up on the church tower, our backs against the parapet, our arms clasped about one another, and I wondered if after all we would die there, of exhaustion and exposure – but then, as though it were a miracle all of our own making, I heard the sound of the church door opening, and Pauly's voice, down below, shouting,

—Caro! Caro! Where are you? Caro, we came in the boat! Grandy rowed us! Caro!

and I shouted back to him,

—Up here, Pauly! It's Sally. We're up here!

I heard his feet hammering on the stairs, coming round and round the spirals, getting closer, and then he burst through the narrow doorway. He ran to Caro. He put his arms around her neck. He kissed her on the forehead, and she started to cry.

x

I left Caro and Pauly at the top of the church tower, and I walked back down the spiral staircase, out of the church, through the churchyard. A hundred yards away, at the water's edge, beside the small rowing boat, Grandy stood, and for a moment I thought that perhaps exhaustion had unhinged me, because, standing straight and with the sun behind him, I saw not the Grandy I had left behind at the high house, who had stooped, and who limped, and had grown old, but the other one, my remembered grandfather who once, when I had run away, had come to find me, and had carried me home across his back.

Caro

I T seems impossible that the rain should have stopped so suddenly, after so long, but this is how I remember it, and I remember the journey back to the high house in bright sunlight, Grandy rowing across water which lay still, now, and quiet. I remember Pauly leaning over the edge of the boat and trailing his hand in the water, making ripples spread out from the tips of his fingers. I remember how his other hand held tightly on to mine, his fingers gripping, although whether it was to stop himself from drowning, or me, I wasn't sure. I remember climbing out of the boat and walking up the slope to the high house which stood, clean, shining in the sunlight, and I remember going through the front door and crawling up the stairs and into bed. And then I slept.

i

I woke again and the world was bright and clear, a pale blue winter sky with a burning sun in it that shone in the air and in the water. There was a fresh, new smell. I went down to the kitchen, where Sally sat in her coat and boots. She had been out to look, she said, and to see what the damage was.

The river had burst its cut, and it ran through the village to meet the sea, which had breached the shingle bank and run a good half-mile onto the land. The dunes were destroyed. The marshes were below the tide. Who knows, she said, what it will look like when the water goes down. If it goes down.

—We're not quite an island,

she said,

—but nearly. The tide pool is safe. The wheel is safe. We can get out onto the heath to the west. The bridge is standing. Francesca planned well.

Sally

T HAT day – the day after the flood – I felt nothing but joy. It was the joy which comes with a clear sky after months of bad weather. It was the joy which comes from the smell of sap and earth. It was the joy which comes from crossing over, and reaching a further shore, which is the joy of ending and of relief. I walked from the high house out into a new-made earth and sang, very loudly, until Pauly, with all his unconcerned directness, came to tell me that it was a very good song I was doing, but not really very good singing, and besides, it was frightening the birds.

i

—Dinner's ready,

I said to Grandy, who was sitting in the chair in his bedroom with a rug over his knees.

—Baked potatoes. Good, solid stuff.

—I'm awfully tired, Sal,

he said, and I noticed that his face was grey, and his eyes looked sunken in.

—Perhaps you could bring me a tray?

—Why not come and sit in the armchair in the kitchen?
I asked,
—and then at least you'll be with us?
But he shook his head, and I brought him a tray with a baked potato on it, which he didn't eat.

ii

Caro took Pauly to the tide pool and he found a stone with two holes right through it. He came back holding it in both his hands, cupped in front of him, as though it were a sacred relic.
—Can I show it to Grandy?
he asked,
—I know he'd want to see.
—Not now,
I said,
—he's resting.
Pauly's face fell.
—He's always resting now.
—Well, he's an old man, and it was a tiring business, rescuing Caro and me. Why don't we find a box for your stone, and you can show it to him later?

iii

Pauly perched on the side of Grandy's bed.
—Do you think it's a very special stone?
he asked Grandy.
—Did you ever see one like it? Another one, I mean?

—Not ever,

Grandy said.

—Now you'd better go and find Caro. I need Sally for a moment.

When Pauly had gone, I watched Grandy's face fall back in on itself. I saw the way his shoulders slumped into the pillow.

—How's your pain?

I asked. He gave a sort of smile.

—So so,

he said.

—I need to go to the bathroom—

and so I draped his arm across my shoulders and pulled him from the bed onto his feet, supporting his weight, trying to match my steps to his, to be gentle, to be kind without condescending, as, very slowly, we made our way to the next room, where I lowered him onto the toilet, and turned my back.

Caro

I T was such a feeling, the first day, to have survived. We had been waiting for the end, and it had come – but it was like cresting a peak only to find, beyond it, the whole bulk of a mountain still to climb. This was the afterwards. We had survived – but must, somehow, continue to do so. Grandy had exhausted himself and now he was in bed, and Sally spent most of her time with him. There was still the garden to be done, and the cooking. Pauly and I went out in the afternoons to collect the driftwood which was left behind as the waters started to sink a little, but by then I had begun to be afraid of the water. I could only think of Pauly, on the marshes, and how I had swung him up in my arms. I could only think how easily he might have drowned, and how it would have been my fault. I tried not to go too close to the edge of the water. At night, I found it hard to sleep. I began to have bad dreams.

i

—We should go to the village,

Sally said, her voice as flat as her face, which was all surface now. I hadn't seen her smile for weeks.

—We need to salvage what we can.

It was not an invitation, but an instruction, and so I didn't say that I was afraid to go. I didn't say that the thought of going inside those drowned houses filled me with horror – that, even though I knew they had been empty, I was afraid that I would find a corpse, its fingers pressed against a window. I went with her and Pauly, one of the big rucksacks on my back, and I tried my best to help, touching what I could bear to, staying as close to the doorways as I could, but knew that I was not doing what Sally wanted, and that it infuriated her.

ii

That was the night Grandy fell. Sally found him in the morning, lying on his bedroom floor. Between us, we managed to get him back into bed, to strip off his clothes and sponge him clean, to put a fresh pair of pyjamas on him while he drifted in and out of consciousness, and sometimes cried out in pain.

—I think his hip is broken,

Sally said, when we were alone in the kitchen.

—What can we do?

I asked, and even as I said it, I knew I had been stupid. Sally looked at me with such contempt.

—What we can,

she said.

Sally

I HAD given Grandy half of one of the vials of morphine, and now his face was smooth. I thought he was asleep, and so I got out the box of antibiotics which I had taken from the barn, and read the instructions. I thought that if, perhaps, I could keep Grandy clear of infection, then his hip might heal enough to let him live. I tried hard not to think what such a life might be.

—I am an old man,

he said, and I saw that his eyes were open, and that he was watching me.

—The end can be fast, or it can be slow, but it can't be avoided. I would rather you kept what you might need.

Every evening for a week we had had the same conversation, and I could feel how much his patience cost him. I had no right to string things out, when he was in such pain. He had not, yet, had to beg, and I couldn't bear the thought of making him do so. I laid my head down on his chest, and heard his heartbeat, slow.

—It is a lot to ask,

he said,

—but it is not, I think, a crime, when it is a mercy.

I closed my eyes, and took his hand in mine.

i

Sometime before dawn, Grandy, drifting for a moment out
of sleep, said,
    —I am so very proud—
    and then he was gone.

Pauly

I REMEMBER the day we buried Grandy in the churchyard, how I watched while Sally and Caro dug the grave, driving their spades again and again into the wet earth. I remember how Caro cried, and Sally didn't. Halfway through they stopped, and we ate a picnic of potato cakes, sitting all three of us together underneath the apple tree. There was bright sunshine, after so much rain. I think we laughed, although I can't remember why. It felt like a release, because we had known since we had come to the high house that it would be the three of us, in the end. Grandy had known. Sally and Caro began to dig again, until the hole was long enough, and deep. Grandy's body was dressed in old clothes, because even then we couldn't bring ourselves to waste what might one day be needed. They had pulled it to the church on the big barrow.

—You don't need to come, Pauly,

Caro had said, and,

—Yes, he does,

Sal answered. She was right, I think. I walked beside them. I saw him tipped into the earth, and buried, and afterwards, back at the high house, I saw Sally go into the barn, and, following her, I watched her slip the box of morphine back onto its shelf.

i

This is mercy, which is the best that we can hope for. We do what we can for one another. We try to be kind.

Sally

S LOWLY, more and more of that which we have salvaged is exhausted, or lost, or starts to rot. Perhaps, if we last long enough, then we will forget what all of it was for – the twisted metal, the burst brick, the plastic which floats, still, across the sea to wash up on the beach – and then, perhaps, some burden will be eased.

Caro

I THINK about all that happened – about how things were, and how they are – and even though the nightmares still come, I can't say that I would rather be dead. I would not rather be dead.

i

In the end, we always choose ourselves. Or our children. We are only here because Francesca couldn't bear the thought of Pauly drowning, but the high house isn't an ark. We aren't really saved. We are only the last ones, waiting.

Pauly

I F I am the last to go, I wonder how long I will stay, after the others are dead. It would not be good to be alone here but worse, I think, to have to make the choice to die without the others there for comfort. I think it will feel very cold. I think it will feel very empty. I imagine going round the house for the last time. I imagine shutting the windows, shutting the doors. The last of us will not be buried. The last will lie here forever, in the high house, which is our sanctuary, and will be our grave.

ACKNOWLEDGEMENTS

Thanks are due to my agent, Lisa Baker, for constant support and encouragement, and for the setting of deadlines; and to my editor, Mark Richards, for making this book better than it was when I wrote it. Thanks also to Paul Miller, for some hypothetical legal advice; to Holly and James Arnott, for telling me about chickens; to Polly and Ada for being quantifiably better than anyone else's children; and to Ben, for pretty much everything else.